IN HER SERVICE

A Collection of Assertive Women
A Mischief Collection of Erotica

T0318052

mischief

Mischief
An imprint of HarperCollins*Publishers*
77–85 Fulham Palace Road,
Hammersmith, London W6 8JB

www.mischiefbooks.com

A Paperback Original 2013

First published in Great Britain in ebook format by
HarperCollins*Publishers* 2012

Copyright
Oppositeland © Charlotte Stein
How Was Your Day? © Valerie Grey
The Perfect Mistress © Monica Belle
A Gift © Willow Sears
Chameleon © Lara Lancey
Land of Pleasure © Kim Mitchell
The Houseboy © Aishling Morgan
Teasing Timmy © Primula Bond
Safe-Word © Ashley Hind

The author asserts the moral right to
be identified as the author of this work

A catalogue record for this book is
available from the British Library

ISBN-13: 9780007553112

Find out more about HarperCollins and the environment at
www.harpercollins.co.uk/green

CONTENTS

Oppositeland
Charlotte Stein

I purposefully pick out the most mundane and unneeded items I can think of, as I stroll around the supermarket with a basket over my arm. Of course, no one pays me the slightest bit of attention because they're all picking out their own mundane and probably unneeded items. Things like the mop they saw on some infomercial or a jar of capers that's on offer they don't want. They'll never use them – the capers, I mean – though really what can I say about that?

I'll never use them either.

Me and Artie, we don't eat capers. We don't eat macaroons either, but they're in my basket too. They're just the most perfect thing to buy to keep my mind on that drifting, unthinking edge, that *I'm completely bored* state of nothingness I don't usually feel when Artie and I walk around the supermarket together. When we do it together, we plan meals and giggle over funny-shaped aubergines, and maybe at some point I'll slip a hand up the back of his jersey because he's just so gorgeous I can't resist him.

Though I suppose you could say I'm resisting him now. This is the ultimate in resisting, really – like a test, I suppose – but it doesn't feel like it, somehow. It feels like something else, instead, though I don't let myself think about it too hard. *Just that little glancing edge of it*, I tell myself, then let my mind wander back to mundane considerations like capers and macaroons and super-mops. I pay for my items and stroll back home, forcing my gaze and my attention over shop-window signs and people I see on the streets, and once there I deliberately put each item away in various newly made spaces.

Though I'd be lying if I said I wasn't aware of Artie's presence.

I am, but it's a peripheral kind of thing. I bustle through the bedroom, collecting things I want to wear after my shower, and I can feel him just burning on the edges of my vision. I'm aware of him twitching and stirring towards the sound and smell of me, and after a moment he allows himself a little faint sigh. I can't tell if it's a discomfited sound or something else, but I don't stop to find out.

I have my shower instead, taking time to remove any scrap of hair on my body and smoothing everything nicely as I go. Once I'm out, I dry myself and rub lotion on my various parts and then after a moment, I slide into the little silky slip thing Artie bought me for my thirtieth birthday.

Of course, it's this action that almost gets me. I think about him running it all over me, bunched in his too-tense fist, telling me how he wanted to buy me something that would make me feel as sexy as he always thinks I am. Something that would feel glorious against my skin and make me near buzz for sex.

And it always does. My nipples stiffen as it flows over them, so cool and buttery soft. All I have to do to know how aroused I am is look down, and see them sticking through the material, dusky-pink and spiky-hard. I'm turned on because of shopping. I'm turned on because Artie's in the bedroom and he's still waiting, waiting, waiting.

When I walk back in there he turns his head blindly, searching me out from beneath the confines of the scarf around his eyes. His breathing is slightly unsteady, but I can't tell if that's because of the promise of things to come, or because he's starting to really feel the effects of the state he's in.

The muscles in his thighs are trembling – I can see them from here. And every now and then he cycles his shoulders backwards and forwards, as though the strain of having his hands tied behind his back then bound to the headboard is getting a bit too much. It's putting pressure on his joints. The leather around his wrists is starting to rub against the tender skin there.

Though I'm not too worried, I have to say, because he's still impossibly hard. Even after all this time – all the shopping and the shower and me getting myself ready – his cock is still sticking right out and almost up, all swollen and slippery at the tip. As I watch, a thin stream of pre-come slides down the length of his stiff shaft and I feel my cunt clench in sympathy.

I don't let him know it, however. I don't say or do anything to him at all. I just walk into the room and stand close enough to let him scent out the lotion on my body, the tang of my shampoo. Of course he doesn't say anything – he just leans forward, slightly, as though he can get at me through sheer force of will. That leather leash straining against the bulk of his big body, the smooth solid rounds of his shoulders standing out starkly through the gloss of his skin as he works against them.

But it's his mouth I like the best. He has a beautiful mouth at the most typical of times – soft and full in his otherwise perfectly masculine face – but now, here, it's even sweeter. His lips are parted and moist, as though he's been constantly licking them just to feel how good and dirty and slick his tongue feels, working over the only point of his body he can reach. And whenever he makes a little sound – a little strained sigh or a pulled-in groan – he ends it with his teeth pressed into that soft flesh.

I'm so wet by this point I can hardly stand it. Even the shower hasn't taken the evidence of my arousal away – the arousal I built up without really thinking about it directly, as I walked around the supermarket and made my way back home – and now it's starting to trickle down my thigh.

But I stiffen my own resolve and keep my voice light and disinterested.

'Did you have a good time while I was gone?' I ask, and his glorious lips move soundlessly around words he can't say. They make me think of other things he could move them around, thicker things, more solid things, and then my clit jerks and more slickness spills down my slippery thighs.

I think I know what I'm going to do to him today. He always says *go further, do more, make it a surprise*, and I think this is going to fulfil those criteria very nicely.

'You haven't been bad, have you?' I ask, and he *mmpfs* in discomfort when I trail a finger down over the solid mass of his body, to the straining stalk between his legs. It jerks upwards when I fondle it, briefly, and then again when I scratch at his tightly drawn up balls. Another second or two of contact and he's going to come, and it isn't just the leaking state of his swollen prick that tells me so.

He's so breathless, and his whole body trembles, tautly. There's a flush all over his cheeks and whenever I get even the slightest bit close, he can't help moaning.

'If you've been bad, I might have to punish you,' I say, but he just strains further forward. As though instead of punishment I said pleasure and instead of tying him I let him go. It's always Oppositeland with him, my Artie.

'But if you've been good,' I tell him, 'if you've been good, I might give you a reward.'

The two are interchangeable, and he knows it. It's why he tenses when he hears me moving towards the bedside cabinet, because I could be doing just about anything. I could be finding something to spank him with, something to whip him with. Once, he begged me to hit him with a belt, right across his back. *Hard*, he'd said, *like you want to mark me, like you want to hurt me.*

And I had obeyed.

But it's always better when it's secret and special and he doesn't quite know what's next. In fact, he's trembling when I return to him. His whole body has drawn taut, and it gets tauter when I go back to him and run the thing I've brought over his only-just-hairy chest.

I think he can tell what it is. It's pretty new and still smells latex-y, because I've hardly used it. Why would I want to use it when I've got his big thick cock at my beck and call, almost the equal of this toy in my hand? I don't even understand why he bought it for me, though I'm getting a clearer picture right now.

His face has gone bright red, despite the fact that almost nothing humiliates him any more. I can grope

6

him right between his legs in the middle of Marks and Spencer's, and nothing happens. He just goes boneless and parts his lips, waiting for more.

'You want it?' I ask, and he groans loudly. Of course he wants it! I should have known. All I have to do is run the head of this thick latex cock over his mouth and he shudders like a struck dog.

He pokes his tongue out and tries to wet his lips, but it just means he ends up inadvertently licking the thing. Or possibly not so inadvertently – I don't know. When I press it to his mouth he won't take it in, but he's not exactly stopping it either. As though most of him is screaming no, but some of him just wants to know what it would be like to take someone's cock in his mouth.

Not that he'd ever admit it. Of course, I've suggested it to him before, in the panting heat of a marathon sex session. Usually when he's on the verge of orgasm and too far gone to care, his cock lodged deep in my pussy and my finger somewhere rude, like between the cheeks of his ass. And he'll squirm and try not to look at me, but I can almost feel what he's thinking – what would it be like? What would it be like to have some guy in his mouth, thrusting until he came?

Like this, I think, and then I order him to suck the vibrator in my hand. As though *I'm* the guy, and I just can't wait for him to do it. I'm hard and eager and wanting it, and he's a wanton slut, almost but not quite willing to give it.

'Yeah, take it,' I say, and he moans around the thick length of the thing. He moans and grimaces and doesn't want to do it, I can tell, but he keeps going nonetheless. He sucks even though I haven't told him to, as though he can taste real flesh and feel real heat and wants nothing better than to please.

And it's so ... so ... oh ...

'Yeah, you like that, baby?' I ask, as my sex swells and more liquid trickles down my thigh. I'm not sure how much more of this I can take, in all honesty, but I'll do it just for him. I always do it just for him. 'Feels good, huh? Feels good taking that big cock in your mouth.'

He squirms and jerks forward, the tip of his cock just skimming the material of my nightie. Though I suppose even so slight a contact must feel like bliss, when you're so close to coming.

Which is why I give him a spank, for his trouble.

'Bad boy,' I tell him and take the sex toy away – like a punishment, I think, though of course I don't know it is one until he actually tries to go after it. His mouth opens and closes, searching and searching for the thing I took away, while my clit jerks and my body thrums and I can't stop myself running a hand over my own nipple.

I have to. He's the one tied up, but I'm the one losing control. I need to dig my fingers in for just a second, feel the flesh of my breast as it gives under the pressure. And once I'm done, I lick the tip of the thing he's just sucked. Just to give myself a little taste. Just to know, for a second, what it's like.

Before I move on to the next stage of the plan.

'Move back,' I tell him, and of course he obeys. He shuffles and wriggles awkwardly, until the leash bows and there's space enough in front of him. Of course, the whole thing is still going to be difficult for him – he can't rely on his arms, after all – but I can't afford to care about that.

Caring is not the point right now.

'Bend over,' I tell him, as abruptly as I can. And though he hesitates, I only think he does because he's considering how best to do this thing. Should he just lean, gingerly? Go face first into the mattress? I don't think there's enough length to the leash to allow the latter, but for a second I think he's going to attempt it.

And then suddenly he's shuffling on the bed again, rear-ranging himself until his legs are spread almost embarrassingly wide, body straining as he attempts to go on all fours – only without the two stabilisers in front. Instead, he's just clinging to the leash behind him, muscles straining to keep him in a rough L-shape, shoulders creaking with the effort.

It's only after he's completely still and in position that I realise I've been holding my breath. Would he do anything, just absolutely anything, if asked him to? If I *told* him to?

I think he would and yet I can hardly believe what I'm seeing. It strikes me hard, in the gut – my husband's almost total willingness to obey – and then once the feeling has dissipated I'm just left with this …

My almost total willingness to push him as far as he can go. It soars through me, so strong suddenly that I'm momentarily stymied. I'm not the cool girl, wandering oblivious around the supermarket. I'm just Clara Henley, clumsy and unsure.

Then less so, when he strains just that little big further and finds the head of the cock I'm still holding, with his mouth.

Of course, it's entirely different when he does it like this. We're on different but familiar levels now, me knelt on the bed in front of him. Him with his face so close to the mattress.

And also to the thing I've inadvertently put in almost the right place. I mean, it's not as though I can avoid the idea. I've done it without thinking, and now it's as though I really *do* have something thick and stiff between my legs.

Something thick and stiff that he's now sucking. Because he definitely is, and I definitely like it. I know I do, even when I don't exactly want to accept it. Words just come to my lips, and they *make* me accept it.

'Yeah, suck my cock, you little bitch,' I say, far fiercer than I was a moment ago. Far gruffer, too, though that sound has almost nothing to do with wanting to feel like a man, in some way. It's because I'm aroused, so aroused at the sight of my husband debasing himself like this, and I just can't keep my voice on the straight and narrow.

It goes up and down and left and right, then drops out altogether when he starts moaning around the thing I'm now holding like a raised fist. Jutting and rude and angry, almost, only pulling back on it when that soaring feeling inside me gets too much.

I could drown in that feeling. I could get lost, and worse – I think he knows it. He wants me to go past that point, but I can't, I can't. This is enough, just this.

Just slapping my husband's face, when he gets too greedy with the cock.

'Enough,' I tell him, while his mouth moves soundlessly around words he doesn't know how to say. Perspiration stands out at his temples, along his hairline, on his upper lip – but it isn't unattractive. Quite the contrary. It spurs me on, in the same way his squirming, heated body does.

Though nothing gets me as good as his response, when I tell him plainly:

'I'm going to fuck you, now.'

It's like I've touched a live wire to his spine. He shoves into the bed even though he knows he'll be punished for that. And he moans so loudly, which he definitely won't be punished for, at all. I could never punish him for something that makes my clit swell and my cunt

11

clench around nothing, every inch of me suddenly right on the edge.

I'm going to come, I realise, calmly. Detached from it, almost. I'm going to come without anything touching me, and all because of the thought of what I'm about to do. I'm going to slick this big cock with oil. And once that's done, I'm going to finger his tight little asshole until he opens up for me.

Then after all of these frankly excruciating stages, I'm going to ease this big thing past that ring of muscle until he begs me for more.

Which he duly does. I knew he would. It's like we're connected too tightly, when we get to this place, every action familiar even though it's absolutely not, in most other ways. My hand feels too slippery – I've used too much oil. I'm conscious, so conscious of hurting him, even though the sight of the plastic sliding past all of his resistance is enough to almost send me over.

And yet that feeling remains. Of knowing him and understanding. It sings in me as he chokes out that I should fuck him so, so hard. *Do it, baby, do it*, he says, but I wait right on the brink. I stay just like that, with the thick shaft only partway inside him. Oil dripping and dripping down over his spread thighs, onto the sheets. Onto me.

Then just as he's ready to beg again, just as I feel it shuddering through me too, I push in hard. I draw the cock I don't have back out again, searching for a rhythm, searching for what he'll like, and oh yes when I find it … when he gasps for me …

'There?' I ask, but I don't need to. He's already shoving back against that feeling, chasing it. He's already saying things I don't dare to, like *ohhh yeah. Make me come, make me feel it, give me that hard fucking thing.*

Of course, I notice that he doesn't use the word cock. But that's OK, because somehow the evasion of it hits me harder. My clit jerks again, just once, as though there's a little string attached from it to the shaft I'm now pumping in and out of him, and I think that's it. I'm going, I'm sure. I'm doing it, without so much as a rub over that swollen little bud.

But no, there's something more to come, yet. Something I need, without even understanding that I do.

It's OK, however. He knows.

'Oh God yeah, baby,' he says, as he works himself back on the thing I'm almost not holding any more. As he shudders, and gets so close, he follows it with other blissful words like: 'You love it, don't you.'

It's not a question, I know. It's permission. Permission to love it, permission to love this. Permission to dig my nails into his back and sob something garbled and frantic like *take it take it take it*, as my orgasm blooms so low and thick in my belly.

It's almost like pain, I think. And it's too all over

the place, too unfocused. It runs riot through my body, glancing over my clit and striking me hard at the tops of my thighs. I almost sink right down onto the bed. It's so strange and not right and good all at the same time.

But I stay up, for him. I keep the twist I'm giving to the cock inside him, until I hear him choke the words out. The ones I can hardly believe myself, even though the thing is still happening.

'Oh Christ,' he says. 'Oh fuck, are you coming? Are you really coming? Ohhhh baby yes, yes. I love you, I love you.'

And then he goes over himself in one big, incredible surge. Body stiffening under its pressure. Near soundless grunts of pleasure throttling their way out of him. Every one of his shudders running all the way down him, and out through me.

Because by this point, I've sprawled all over his back. I can hardly help it – every bone in my body seems to have turned to soup. I'm wrung out, done in, turned upside down. Of course I am. I'm in Oppositeland, where orgasms happen without touching and he gets fucked, not me.

Where instead of saying *I despise you for making me wait like that*, he murmurs, low and sweet:

'You're so good to me, my lovely girl. So good in every way.'

I'm not, though. Sometimes I'm thoughtless, and

impatient. Occasionally I cry without warning, and won't let him comfort me. Hell, there are even times when I *can't* let him comfort me, when I can't let him in, when I don't know what to say a second after he's told me he loves me.

But I can do this.

For him, I can be the person I pretend I'm not.

How Was Your Day?
Valerie Grey

Made sure everything was in place and did a final check
of the things I would need: a blindfold, a feather, a bowl
of ice, a candle, a lighter and a rubber glove – just in case.

This thought made my stomach tighten and for a
moment and I wondered if I was making a terrible
mistake.

The sound of a car pulling into the drive cut that
apprehensive thought off before I could change my mind.
How long would it take to put all this away and do the
dishes? Too long – *oh*, one look at the sink full of this
morning's dishes and she'd know *something* was suspi-
cious. It was the one thing she'd asked me to do before
she left.

Asked?

In her own way she *asked*: 'Make sure the dishes get
done before I get home tonight. Do you *understand*?'

16

'Yes,' had been my simple reply.

Oh, yes, I understood perfectly well. I knew that if they weren't done I would pay for that transgression. I didn't know how the consequences would occur but I had no doubts that they would, indeed, occur. *Of that I had no doubt.* And now it was too late to question the intelligence of the decision I had made not to do them. They still sat stacked in the same neat piles they had been in this morning. I could almost swear they were taunting me now. Now, when even they must know it was too late to change my mind.

The sound of a key unlocking the door invaded the thunderous silence of my own thought. Holding my breath, I watched as the figure of my lover filled the doorway. She had a way of making me forget even to breathe and my heart fluttered like a princess catching sight of the royal queen in the nude.

Seeing me standing in the entrance with signs of obvious apprehension made her raise an eyebrow inquisitively. A gleam of curiosity flickered in the depths of her hazel eyes before being shadowed by a mask of indifference.

'Well, well, what has made *you* so eager to greet me and yet so hesitant to speak, little one?' she asked softly.

It was a softness of voice that could be misleading. Now more than ever I wanted desperately to have just a few more minutes to do the damn dishes and how I anticipated pleasing her as well. Words were stuck in my throat. I felt my mouth open and close again but no sound came out.

She knew more by my silence than by my words that I had not done as she had asked. She was not going to let me off easily. She was not going to fill in the blanks for me; she was going to demand that I admit to my sin. And she was going to draw out the anticipation as long as she could. It was a gift she had – to say and do nothing and let me torture myself in the process.

Slowly, she took off her coat, hung it in the hall closet and said, 'So, how was *your* day?'

My day? *How was my day?* How could she ask me that? What does she mean, how was my day? Images of how I spent the seemingly endless hours of my day flashed through my mind like a trailer for a new TV show.

This was going to be worse than I had imagined.

My day was spent preparing myself for what I knew was going to be a very satisfying night with you. My day was spent cleaning, dusting, vacuuming, scrubbing, showering and shaving to make everything perfect for you. The way you like it. My day was spent trying desperately to avoid the kitchen sink so as not to be tempted to do the one chore you asked of me. My day was spent wondering how you would react when you saw the dishes still piled up in the sink from this morning. My day was spent carefully planning and calculating this exact moment. But never once in the course of my day

*did I actually expect that I would have to tell you that
I didn't do the one task you had required of me. Never
once during the entire day. How do I tell you all that?*

Not knowing how to do so I said simply: 'Fine.'

'*Fine?* Tell me more. Tell me what you did today.
Tell me *everything*,' she demanded. Nervously, I began
rattling off all the chores I had done during the day.
While reciting the events of the day I began to walk with
her to the bedroom where I untied her boots, removed
them and set them neatly by the door. I almost added
this to my list of events for the day but thought better
of it and refrained.

'Is that all?' she said.

This was the moment I had been waiting for all day.
I wanted the chance to tell her what I had really been
doing all day.

'No,' I said.

I didn't have the courage to look at her when I finished
the rest of the sentence, so I stated the remainder of my
memorised speech to her sock-clad feet.

'I also prepared myself to show you how much I
adore you. If you will only allow me to show you this,
Mistress, it will hopefully be worthwhile for you. *Please.*'
I finished in a rush.

Surprised at this unusual change of topic she assessed
me for a moment, then slowly inclined her head once to
grant me permission to continue.

Thrilled at this opportunity to please her, I began to unbutton her shirt slowly, babbling about how much I had looked forward to her coming home and how eager I was to make her happy.

Her shirt was completely removed and I placed my hands on the buttons of her jeans.

Before I could continue she put her hands forcefully on top of mine to stop me. She said, 'You will please me only when you are naked before me *and not before.*'

I stood before her and began to unbutton my shirt and let it slip gently over my shoulders and slide down my back to the floor. Shivering from the sensations of the starched cotton gliding over my soft skin, I unbuttoned my jeans and turned so that when I slid them down I would be bent over with my panty-clad ass in the air toward her.

A soft hiss of breath told me that she appreciated the view.

I stepped carefully out of each leg of my jeans before slowly turning back toward her.

Looking deep into her eyes, I unhooked my bra and crossed my arms over my chest to pull the arm straps down. She could tell me to strip but I could decide how slowly I wanted to reveal myself to her.

Dropping my bra on the pile of clothes already on the floor, I thrust my chest proudly forward toward her. I knew she liked my breasts. She would often come up to squeeze them or to pinch the nipples just to watch them pucker and strain into her palm.

My growing excitement and the coolness of the air now caused them to become tiny hard beads. I wondered if she had noticed yet, so I cupped one breast in each hand and pinched the tiny nipples so that they jutted out toward her more.

She noticed.

I heard her deep, low growl and knew I was pushing the limits of how far she would let me play this taunting game with her. I quickly moved my fingers down to the waistband of my lavender panties, edged them under the tight elastic and began slowly pushing them down the length of my thighs. This time I bent forward to cover as much of my body as possible, hoping to draw this delicious moment out for one more heartbeat.

I knew her gaze would be fixed on my now free-swinging pendulous breasts as they drew toward the floor. I finally stood up, stepped out of my panties, left them where they fell and allowed her to gaze on my now fully naked body.

I began walking toward her; her eyes were still on my rock-hard nipples. When I reached the bed I again placed my hand on the buttons of her jeans and began to pull them slowly open. She stood up so that I could drag them down to the floor without delay. Kneeling at her feet, I pulled her jeans completely off and before I

21

had the chance to stand again she grabbed me by the back of my hair and tugged on it, hard enough to make my eyes water.

She growled, 'You are *mine*, little one.'

As if I needed to be reminded.

As if it weren't already in my every thought?

Even though she hadn't phrased it as a question, I answered her with an immediate:

'Yes, Mistress, I am all yours. *Always*.'

Forever.

She released my hair and allowed me to continue my ministrations. I finished undressing her and asked if she would grant me the further liberty of blindfolding her.

'For what purpose?' she demanded.

'Simply for the purpose of further pleasing you, Mistress. I wish to show you what I feel but I am still a bit … nervous.'

She nodded once. 'Good. Nervous will keep you in line, but remember that I will allow it only this once.'

She climbed onto the huge captain's bed, lay down there with her hands propped behind her head, and waited for me to continue.

Yes, she would grant me certain liberties, but she would not make obtaining them any easier.

I climbed onto the bed after her and reached down behind the bed to where I had hidden my 'stash' of materials earlier in the day. Carefully, so as not to disturb her, I again knelt over the side of the bed and picked up the feather. Not knowing where to start, I began at the most logical place: her face. I felt her slight twitch at the initial contact of the feather on her skin. Slowly I traced every curve and hollow of her beautiful face.

Lovingly, I watched as the feather traced the path that I wished my tongue could follow. But I knew if I gave in now it would be over too quickly. And I wanted this to last. Gently, I switched from a gliding motion to a quick tapping one and tapped a path down her neck to her shoulders. Without warning I replaced the feather with an ice cube. I heard her startled gasp and then nothing.

She returned to reserved silence. With one hand I continued the chilling assault on her upper body, from shoulders to breasts and back. With the other I carefully prepared the next sensation tool: the candle. I could see the wet path the ice had left along her skin. I could see a hint of goose bumps on her flesh, the only indication that she was cold, for her voice would give nothing away.

I lifted the ice cube off her body and cooed, 'You are cold. Here, let me warm you,' and I lifted the candle and tilted it directly over her taut nipple.

A sharp cry and a muffled gasp were the only indications that she had noticed the difference.

Confident now, I continued to leave a trail of hot wax followed by a soothing drop of water from the ice cube along her entire torso, focusing on her now rigid nipples and tender breasts. Fascinated, I watched as the wax created miniature sculptures on her erect nipples.

But it was not enough.

I wanted more.

I set aside the candle and the ice so that I could test out the sensations I alone could create. Nothing artificial: simply flesh, tongue, teeth. I couldn't imagine ever being sated by this woman.

My Mistress, my lover, my everything.

I began to nip at the soft flesh of her inner thighs. Again startled by the path I had taken, but apparently eager to experience more, she parted her thighs to allow me entrance to her wetness. But I refused to allow her to finish so quickly. With more strength than I knew I had, I lifted her left side and rolled her onto her stomach. She struggled to regain control, but I was too heady to stop.

Lying fully along the length of her body I whispered into her ear, 'Please. Not yet. Let me first show you what it is to be taken in the same way you take me. Let me feel your power while you feel my pleasure.'

Ceasing her struggles, she growled into the pillow that she was allowing me one final chance before she called an end to this game. I agreed quickly. Sitting up, I could for a moment only gasp appreciatively at the sight of her prone body. The muscles of her back were tense from anticipation. I ran my fingers lightly along these to ease her stress.

My eyes followed a path lower to the tight curve of her ass.

I remembered the feel of that ass beneath my fingertips. Ah, yes, the ass that would tighten with each thrust of her hips as she drove a cock relentlessly inside me. A cock that would find itself imbedded in my wet pussy and claim it as its own. My hands would dig into her flesh, aching to feel the heat I knew was inside her. My nails cut tiny half moons into the supple flesh of her ass as I grabbed her, trying to pull her deeper inside of me.

I could smell her musky scent as she began to get wet from my touch. This must be what she feels when she is inside of me: this power, the thrill. Now I knew why she took me with such passionate force. And again I wanted more. I scored a path with my nails down the length of her back from shoulders to ass and watched in fascination as the marks went from glowing white to a dark pink colour. Again I scored the same path, this time digging in harder until angry red marks began to rise in long thin welts.

Mistress was surprisingly quiet. Her body flinched under my assault, but I wanted still more. I wanted to hear her cry out the same way I cried out when she fucked me so expertly. Angry and frustrated that this most recent tactic hadn't gotten such a response, I leaned down and bit her right shoulder. She groaned deep in her throat which merely excited me further. I leaned back and saw the perfect circle of dents my teeth had left in her skin.

Beautiful.

For a start.

Grabbing her hips with my nails, I bent down and sunk my teeth deep into her left shoulder. I could feel the soft tissue of muscle give way beneath my sharp incisors. This time I got a definitive reaction. She forcefully thrust her head and her ass into the air and moaned in pain. And pleasure? Who would have thought? Wasn't I the only one who enjoyed the pinching sensation of being bitten?

The scent of her pussy drew me down to where her ass and thighs met in a diamond patch of wetness. Groaning, I thrust my tongue deep into her pussy to drink in as much of her come as possible. She thrust her ass into the air to give me further access to her pussy and finally deigned to speak to me.

'Now *there's* the little slut I'm used to. I wondered how long it would take you to tire of your game and finally put your tongue where it belongs.'

I was a slave to her cunt.

She dictated to me exactly how and where to put my tongue and fingers and how to fuck her properly.

'That's right, little one, keep working my pussy. And I want your fingers on my clit nonstop. Do you *hear* me? If you stop rubbing my clit even for *one second* or if you pull your little slut tongue out of my pussy once *without my permission* I will get up and leave you here. I will tie you down with nothing but my wetness on your chin to remind you of me. Do you want that? Do you want me to take my pussy away from you?'

She tormented me.

All I could do was groan and attempt a muffled 'yes' while trying to keep my tongue thrusting into her hot, wet pussy and working my fingers furiously on her clit. Desperate to have her continue to allow me to tongue-fuck her, I sucked hard on her cunt and pounded her clit back and forth until I began to feel her tighten.

'Not yet, little one. I'm going to make you *work* for me to come. First you are going to feel my pussy juice with your fingers inside me and you can keep your greedy tongue occupied by licking my ass. And if you do a very good job at tonguing my ass and finger-fucking me I will let you come when I am done.'

I couldn't do anything but mumble 'yes' before she had thrust her rounded ass into my face and demanded: 'Give it your tongue. I want it hard and tight. *Now!*'

Thrusting my fingers into her now dripping wet pussy and my tongue into her tight asshole, I could feel my own clit tingling and begging for release.

She ordered: 'Don't you dare come until I do, bitch, or you will not be allowed to suck my cunt for a month! You just keep finger-fucking me good and give me that tongue all around my ass like the good little slave you are.'

She breathlessly began to force herself back onto my tongue and fingers hard. She increased her rhythm until she was fucking herself onto me. I was nothing but her personal 'ass and cunt dildo' and I loved every minute of it.

My own cunt was clenching hard trying to achieve the release it ached for, but I continued to turn my focus from my own tingling pussy to that of my mistress. I could feel her tightening around my fingers. She reached back to hold my head in place as she thrust back onto me to push my tongue and fingers in deeply one final time before she shouted out her release. Sweating from holding my own orgasm, I could only shake and hold onto her tightly until I could bring my breathing under control.

'You really are a greedy slut, aren't you? I bet you could come just from tonguing my ass, couldn't you?'

I could only pant, 'Yes, Mistress.'

'Prove it!' she yelled. 'You may lick my ass, but you may not touch either my cunt or your own.'

Grabbing hold of her hips, I began to rock myself into a fucking motion with my tongue penetrating and withdrawing from her ass rhythmically. Picturing how she always withdrew her dildo from my pussy almost to the point of pulling completely out and then thrusting hard and deep into me again, I mimicked this same pattern with my tongue and her ass.

Each time my tongue would push into her ass, my hips would thrust down onto the bed and rub my own clit against the harsh texture of the blanket that was still on the bed. How I wished I had a cock for just one minute and could feel the tight ridges of her ass muscles clenching around my hard erection as I forced it deep inside her virginal ass. If only I could force my tongue to swell and fill her tighter and deeper. I wanted to crawl inside her. I wanted to feel her pussy from the inside out. I wanted to fuck her like she fucks me.

'Fuck me with your tongue. Feel me suck you deep into me. I feel you ready to come. Yes, come for me, little one. That's it – oh, you are *so ready* to come for me, aren't you?'

I could only grab her hard, pull her deeper onto me and thrust my clit one final time against the bed before I felt the deep and violent explosion rock me. Crying out, I stretched up trying to ride out the crest of the wave as it washed over me. She didn't give me time to think before she reached back to grab me by my hair and pulled me up to where she lay. She thrust me onto my back and demanded that I tell her to whom I belonged.

'You, Mistress,' I said. 'There is only you.'

'That's right,' she said, 'and I don't *ever* want you to forget it.'

She forced three fingers into my still quivering wet cunthole and began to finger-fuck me hard. I rode her fingers and grabbed her ass to pull her harder and deeper into me. She didn't give me time to breathe as she thrust her tongue into my mouth and began the same assault on my mouth that her hand was doing to my pussy.

Again the crest of an orgasm overtook me so force-fully that I instinctively grasped at her wrist in a silent plea for her to cease her torment and allow me to ride out this orgasm gently.

My nails dug deep into her wrist.

I could feel her pulse beating erratically beneath my fingertips.

My cunt was desperately sucking on her fingers, seeking a final stretch of closure from the most recent orgasm.

'I can feel your pussy sucking my fingers like it was its favourite cock,' she said, 'but it is your mouth that should be sucking my cock dry.'

She pulled her fingers from my sopping pussy and pressed them to my lips.

'Open up, little one, and taste your sweet cunt on my fingers. Lick them dry like the good little slut girl you are.'

I sucked on her juice-soaked fingers. I drew them deep into my throat and thrust my tongue in between each finger to make sure I had sucked off every bit of it.

'Good girl,' she said, 'now go bring me my pants and pick up the clothes you so *sloppily* threw on the floor in your greedy haste to please me.'

I brought her jeans from the floor and turned to pick up my own pair that I had tossed next to them.

So absorbed was I in my task that I had neither seen her remove the belt from the loops of her jeans nor heard the soft whistle of the leather as it swung through the air in an arc toward me. It was not until I felt the sharp sting and heard the loud crack of the soft leather on my ass that I remembered that I had not told her about the dishes I hadn't done that day. But she had remembered.

Remembered with a vengeance, apparently, from the feel of the sudden heat on my ass. I stood up and turned toward her with shock in my eyes.

'I can see you thought I had forgotten, *hadn't* you?' she said.

I could do nothing but shudder.

'Did you think I would forget with your little game that I gave you a task to complete and that you had completely disregarded my request today?'

'N-no, I just ...'

'You just *what?* Don't try to get yourself out of it now. You knew what you would get if you didn't have them done today, didn't you?'

'Yes, Mistress, but I tried to explain ...'

'No buts!' She cut me off. 'None, that is, *but yours*. Now, get over here, put your hands up in the air and spread your legs out. Take your punishment like a good little girl. You don't want to make this any worse than it already will be, do you?'

Numb, I walked over to where she stood, put my hands up over my head and spread my legs out in a solid stance.

She grabbed my wrists and held them together over

31

my head so I wouldn't be tempted to try to cover ass with them or to ease the pain in any way. Without warning she began the assault on my ass and thighs, all the while reciting my transgressions. I could do nothing but dance from one foot to the other while listening to the litany of my sins fall from her lips. I had not only not done the dishes, I had purposely disobeyed a direct request, refrained from telling her that I had disobeyed that same request, overstepped my bounds to demand that I be allowed to please her, plotted a seduction without asking permission first, come without asking permission, and stopped her hand from continuing to thrust into my pussy during the last orgasm because I had decided I was done. At this last sin she began a furious rhythm with the belt on my now fiery ass.

'*Whose* pussy is it?' she demanded.

'Yours, Mistress,' I managed between gasps of pain.

'That's *right*. And *who* decides when it comes?'

'You do,' I replied quickly, before gritting my teeth against the continued onslaught of leather on my ass.

'And who decides when it has had enough?'

'You do, Mistress!' I sobbed.

'That's right. And until you learn that lesson you will sleep with your hands tied to the bed posts so you can't touch your cunt at night when I am asleep. That way you will remember *whose* cunt it is! Do you *understand* me, little bitch?'

Yes. I did.

She placed my hands on the edge of the bed, forcing me into a prone position to continue the whipping. She then released the bottom part of the belt so that each swing brought it up under my ass to snap squarely on my now engorged clit. Each blow was torture to live through but afterward my ass instinctively rose up higher to meet each one.

Quivering and barely able to stand up, I sobbed, 'Please, Mistress, forgive me. Please!'

Another rain of sharp slaps answered my plea along with her vicious demands of 'Whom do you live to please?'

It was all I could do to gain enough breath to gasp 'You' in response.

'That's *right*,' she said, 'and who has the power to make you come or leave you right here right now with your ass on fire, your pussy soaked through, and your clit swollen and throbbing and begging for release?'

'You,' I said through clenched teeth.

I tried not to think about the fire that had since turned into a low intense heat in my ass and thighs and pussy. Blue fire, I thought. It looks harmless and beautiful but it was the most intense heat known to man. It could destroy you and leave you wondering what had happened. This is how I imagined my mistress now: deceivingly calm and beautiful.

This was how I best knew her: powerful and torrential. *Blue fire*.

She tightened her hold on the belt now, so only a few inches of it was being used to whip me. Furiously, she lashed out and focused her energy on my clit alone. It was so filled with blood, I thought it would explode. Harder and harder she whipped my tender, swollen clit until I thought I could stand it no more.

'Please, Mistress,' I said.

'Please *what*, whore?'

'Please may I come? Please! Oh, Mistress, please, *I am begging you*,' I cried in distress. I could feel myself slipping into the deep warmth of an oncoming orgasm and I pleaded again.

The heat in my clit was so intense, I thought it would spontaneously combust.

I knew in just a few more seconds it would explode without my consent.

'Yes, little one, I feel you. I feel your clit so hard and on fire from me torturing it. I know that I have your clit at the end of my whip begging, aching to be released from its confines. I know that it is ready to come. And I am ready for it to come. Let your clit explode for me now. *Come hard for me, little one*.'

She reared back and swung the belt down for one final hard smack onto the centre of my clit, causing it to explode inside of me. That final blow shattered me into a thousand tiny pieces, causing me to fall onto the bed where I lay for long moments breathing in short shallow gasps for air.

When I was finally able to breathe normally again I stood up and looked around. Mistress was gone. She had taken her clothes with her to wherever she had gone. I bent to pick up my discarded clothes.

On my way to the kitchen to do the dishes finally, I passed by the bathroom and an odd gleam caught my eye.

She had written a note on the bathroom mirror for me.

I expect the bed to be made by the time I get home. Do you understand, little slut?

Oh, yes, Mistress, I understand; I understand perfectly what not to do.

The Perfect Mistress
Monica Belle

David got down on his knees and hung his head. His hands were crossed behind his back, his knees slightly apart, the pose he had been ordered to adopt when waiting to serve his Mistress. Madame Venus ignored him as she took a bite of the chocolate-topped doughnut he had bought her, then a swallow of coffee. The lines of her dark, handsome faced creased into a frown.

'This has no sugar in it.'

'Sorry, Mistress, but ...'

'Shut up, you little piece of dirt. Did I say you could speak?'

David shook his head. She extended one booted foot, pressed it against his chest and pushed. He rolled back onto the floor as she extended one heavy arm, holding out the cup of coffee. He stayed down, making no effort to defend himself beyond closing his eyes as she tipped the

36

mug sideways, to pour out hot liquid onto his body, deliberately soaking his hair and the tight cotton underpants that were his only garment. Only when she'd allowed the final drop to splash onto the bare skin of his chest did she speak.

'Make me another coffee, and make it properly. Then you can clean up this mess.'

He scrambled up again, but instead of going to make the coffee as he had been ordered he resumed his kneeling position, this time with one hand raised, the signal that he wanted permission to speak. Madame Venus drew a heavy sigh.

'Yes, what is it?'

David found his voice cracking as he replied.

'Please, Mistress, may your humble slave respectfully suggest that you should ... might benefit from, and I'm only thinking of your health, Mistress, but ... maybe you should lose a little weight? So I thought, maybe, no sugar in your coffee, and that's a low calorie doughnut, with ... with ...'

He trailed off, looking up at her from his position at her feet, kneeling in the pool of spilt coffee. She was sat on a bar stool at the kitchen work surface, her legs crossed so that the toe of one of her highly polished black boots was within inches of his face. The boots were knee high and fastened with criss-crossed laces he'd tied himself as he helped her dress. Fishnet stockings showed above her boot tops, covering full, dark thighs all the way up to the hem of the black leather miniskirt that encased her hips. A tightly laced corset held in the bulge of her stomach and lifted her huge breasts into prominence. The sight left him weak at the knees, with his cock straining uncomfortably within the chastity device he was obliged to wear whenever he visited her. But for all the awe inspired by her body there was simply too much of it for the perfection her craved.

David knew how the perfect Mistress should look. He had devoured literature on female domination ever since the awakening of his submissive sexuality. A true Mistress was tall and powerful, and Madame Venus was all of that, but the ideal was also slender, with a tiny, wasp waist in contrast to feminine but elegant hips and a full, firm chest. Madame Venus had breasts so huge he could barely support them properly with two hands, along with a bottom so well fleshed that when he was being queened he couldn't even see, let alone breathe. Everything about her made him ache with need, but it was simply too much and he knew that in order to excite the envy of his friends as well as answer his sexual needs she would need to lose three or maybe four stone in weight.

She hadn't answered him, apparently struck dumb by his sheer insolence, but he was determined to persevere.

'I mean no disrespect, Mistress, but ...'

'Shut up! You ... you ...'

She was lost for words, but not action. One hard thrust from the sole of her boot and he was back on the floor, grovelling in the spilt coffee as he babbled out apologies and yet continued to press his point.

'I'm sorry, Mistress. Please forgive your humble slave, but I'm only thinking of your health, and ... and ...'

He broke off with a sharp cry. She had stood up, tugged her skirt high and pulled the lacy black panties beneath to one side, and without any warning at all let go a thick, golden stream of urine. It splashed against his chest and into his face, filling his open mouth to overflowing, and lower, to soak his underpants, leaving the shape of his chastity device showing beneath the wet cotton. He grovelled down, shaking as he was slowly and carefully pissed on, his body soiled from head to toe, until she had shaken off the last few golden droplets into his hair.

'Pants down, face on the floor, you can lick that up while I beat you.'

David hurried to get into position, lapping at the mess on the floor even as he stripped himself behind and lifted his haunches. She pulled open a drawer and took out a heavy wooden stirring spoon, which he knew from experience hurt every bit as much as her more elaborate toys. Normally he was spanked by hand first, but this time she didn't bother and smacked the spoon down on his naked, sodden flesh with the full strength of her arm. He screamed, but he was licking at the floor again in seconds and continued to do so as he was beaten and lectured on his disrespect.

Madame Venus made her points well, punctuating her remarks with hard slaps to David's buttocks. She reminded him that he was her property, to do with as she pleased, that he had no right to criticise her in any way whatsoever, that her word was law and her body an object of worship. He barely heard. His mouth was full of the mess from the floor and his buttocks ablaze, his cock straining in its confinement as his excitement rose. Finally he was pushed over the edge, spunk erupting from his agonised cock despite the restraint.

* * *

For two weeks David lived a life of constant frustration and growing fear. His attempt at persuading Madame Venus to become his ideal had ended with him being thrown out of her house with his underwear still soiled and soggy beneath his clothes, his buttocks a mass of bruises and his chastity device tightened another two notches. Madame Venus held the key.

At first the situation had been uncomfortable but highly arousing, so much so that even the awkward process of cleaning himself up had left him shaking with desire. He had rung Madame Venus, intending to thank her for the experience, apologise for his behaviour and perhaps ask if she had thought about what he'd said. His number had been blocked. For days he waited before trying her number again, telling himself he was being punished and that she would call him when he had served his sentence. He remained blocked.

She had ordered him to stay away from her house, but after a week his resolve broke. He went to her, expecting to be beaten for his insolence, only to find the curtains drawn and the door firmly locked. Listening through the letterbox, he could hear the sound of her voice and another, mingled with laughter that hurt more than any whip or cane. As he walked back towards the bus stop through chilling rain he was again telling himself that he was being punished, that it was just, and that it would all be worthwhile in the end. His confidence was superficial, and hid a growing concern, that she had not only abandoned him, but would leave him in chastity, which meant that eventually he would be forced to make an agonisingly embarrassing trip to hospital to have his device removed.

His suspicions grew stronger across the second week. Every day he called her and every day he sneaked round to her house, to meet with the same wall of silence. He began to experience bursts of panic and long periods of misery and self-recrimination, until the strongest of his emotions was despair and only in an occasional fit of optimism would he feel that she would eventually let him back into her life, and take on board his advice.

Two weeks to the day she had thrown him out his phone rang. When he heard her voice he went straight to his knees, begging forgiveness and offering himself up for any punishment she chose to give, just as long as he could visit her. She took her time over her decision, openly enjoying his hurt and frustration, before telling him to present himself at her house the following day, in ordinary clothes but with frilled pink knickers underneath, a touch he always found particularly humiliating.

He obeyed, counting the minutes until he was permitted into her presence and arriving at her house nearly an hour early. She made him wait in the street, either indifferent or amused by his embarrassment under the curious stares of passers-by. Finally he was admitted, and fell to his knees the moment the door had closed behind him, then grovelled down further still, to kiss at the bright red heels she was wearing, only for her to draw back.

'Don't you dare slobber all over my new shoes, you revolting little worm. Right, strip, and for your sake I hope you're wearing your panties.'

'Yes, Mistress. Just as you ordered, Mistress.'

He was undressing even as he spoke, hurrying off his outer clothes and putting them to the side as he was supposed to do. She watched, not speaking, until he was in nothing but the ridiculous knickers.

'What a sight! OK, get in here, crawling.'

David obeyed, following on his hands and knees as she

strode to the back of the house, never so much as bothering to glance back. He knew full well where she was going – to the small but well equipped dungeon at the rear of the house, where he could be given the treatment he felt he so richly deserved. She stopped at the door, turning to step on his back and force him down to the ground as she spoke.

'You, scum, do not deserve to be my slave.'

He shook his head, struggling to speak as his face was pushed into the carpet.

'No, Mistress.'

'What you deserve is to be dismissed, kicked right out of my life, for good. Unfortunately I doubt that would teach you the lesson you need to learn, would it?'

'I … I don't know, Mistress. I don't understand.'

'I don't suppose you would, idiot. Your trouble is that you still think of yourself the way you were brought up, as a man, in a male-dominated society. You think you're entitled to attitudes and opinions that you're just not, and that I ought to fall in line with that. No, don't protest, just think, if you can think with that walnut-sized brain of yours.'

'Yes, Mistress. I'm sorry, Mistress.'

'No you're not, but you will be. Come inside.'

She had opened the dungeon door and David crawled forward, frightened for the pain he knew would be coming but urgent for exactly what he feared. As he came through the door Madame Venus spoke again.

'Meet Mistress Vixen.'

David looked up, his eyes coming wide and his mouth dropping open in astonishment as he took in the vision in front of him. The first thing he saw were her shoes, black high-heeled boots in shiny patent leather reaching just to her ankles before they gave way to sheer nylon stockings with a seam at the back. Her legs rose high, impossibly long and slender, smooth and sculpted, a true vision that ended at the hem of an enticingly short dress. That too was black, but heavy silk and beautifully cut to accentuate a figure as fine as anything he had seen in the best of domination cartoons or his own fevered masturbation fantasies. Her hips were svelte and elegant, her waist a tiny, waspish constriction made more prominent still by a black leather belt, her breasts high and heavy and round, the perfect size and shape. A short jacket of the same rich silk covered her shoulders and upper arms, while glossy black gloves reached to her elbows and a neat black hat was perched on her abundant hair, with a veil half obscuring her face. Her features were beautiful but sharp, her expression haughty but faintly amused, as if by the antics of a pet dog, as David grovelled down at her feet. Finally she spoke.

'Well, aren't you going to thank your Mistress?'

'Thank you, Mistress! Thank you for deigning to speak to me, thank you … thank you …'

'Not me, you little ingrate, your Mistress.'

David realised his mistake, too late. Madame Venus was looking down at him, her eyes ablaze as she spoke.

'Why you ungrateful little tick! I thought that would be your reaction, you piece of scum, and all this time you've been calling me your Mistress! How dare you!'

David turned to her, abasing himself, but even as he began to mumble out his apologies he knew in his heart that it should be Mistress Vixen he truly belonged to. Madame Venus was wonderful, and he had no intention of giving up his right to serve her, but Mistress Vixen was sheer perfection. For a moment he wondered if he dare explain his feelings, in the hope that Madame Venus might recognise her place as number two to her more glamorous friend, but he knew full well that he would only get himself into deeper trouble. It was Mistress Vixen who spoke again.

'You were right, a typical nasty little boy. Whatever is to be done with him?'

Madame Venus gave an angry snort and reached out to push David over with her toe. He went down, pressing himself to the carpet in utter submission, not daring to hope that the two women might choose to dominate him together, preferably with Mistress Vixen calling the shots. Madame Venus gave him another prod with her toe.

'It's difficult to really punish him these days. He's used to beatings and he loves to be pissed on. I've had him in chastity too, for as long as it's safe, but if he gets too excited he'll spunk up anyway. There are only a few things I haven't tried, your speciality included.'

Mistress Vixen gave a soft chuckle.

'We'll get to that in a while, shall we? Meanwhile, it might be amusing to milk him.'

'Be my guest.'

Madame Venus stepped back, seating herself on a padded whipping stool over which David had spent many hours. She had taken a long, stiff-shafted riding whip from the rack of implements on the wall and used it to give a him a few firm flicks on his back and buttocks, just hard enough to sting, then sat back, smiling faintly.

Mistress Vixen had also taken some gear from the rack, a length of soft, smooth cord and a yellow plastic dog bowl with the word Fido on one side. She put the bowl on the ground, then beckoned to David.

'Get up, you pathetic creature. Crawl to me.'

He hastened to obey, mesmerised by her air of easy power as much as her beautiful body and astonished that she should suggest something that might be demeaning but hardly qualified as a punishment. Mistress Vixen waited until he was in position before giving the dog bowl a fastidious nudge with her foot, to leave it directly under his cock where it hung down in the rounded bulb of his chastity device, the flesh already painfully hard against the plastic. She gave a faint nod as she saw.

'I see what your problem is. He's too small, so when he starts to get stiff he can rub himself off. You need the new version, which comes in a wider variety of sizes.'

'I'll make him buy one, thanks.'

David felt an immediate flush of pleasure to hear Madame Venus defer to Mistress Vixen, but took care to hide his reaction. The key was thrown out, to land on the carpet near his head. He quickly released himself, unable to restrain a sigh of pleasure and relief as his cock and balls came free. Mistress Vixen laughed to see his reaction and extended one immaculate boot to waggle his cock and balls from behind.

'That's a pretty pathetic specimen, isn't it? Gloves, please.'

Madame Venus passed across the box of disposable rubber gloves and again David thrilled to see Mistress Vixen in charge. His cock was already half-stiff, and continued to grow as he surreptitiously watched from the corner of one eye while Mistress Vixen pulled on a rubber glove over her black one. By the time she'd pulled a chair up he was sporting a nearly full erection and was unable to stop himself sighing in pleasure as she took hold. He got a smack for his pains, but she continued to work on him, picking up the cord she'd chosen and wrapping it around his genitals.

A few deft twists and his cock and balls had been put in bondage, his scrotum stretched out by several wraps of twine and his straining erection likewise. As she tied him off, he was already groaning in ecstasy and scarcely able to believe that such a beautiful, dominant woman was treating him so intimately. As her gloved hand closed on his cock he was spilling out his thanks between gasps and sighs.

'Thank you, Mistress Vixen, thank you. You are perfect ... truly perfect, a true, naturally dominant woman ... like Madame Venus, and thank you too, Madame, for permitting me to experience this when I am so unworthy ... so unworthy to even look at a woman like you, Mistress Vixen, so unworthy!'

He broke off, no longer able to speak coherently for the ecstasy flooding through him as she began to masturbate him into the dog bowl. In just seconds he was having trouble holding himself back, his excitement near impossible to control after so long in chastity. His whole body was shaking and he'd begun to sob in raw emotion for the feelings building up inside him, but still he fought to hold off the moment of no return, prolonging his ecstasy, until Mistress Vixen spoke once more.

'Turn around, you pathetic little slut.'

David's eyes came wide, to find himself staring at her from just a couple of feet away, where she had squatted down to milk his cock. She had pulled her dress low, exposing the perfect twin globes of her breasts, round and heavy and bare, each tipped with a stiff red nipple.

At the same instant she began to pull faster on his shaft. It was all too much. He came with a groan, gout after gout of spunk erupting into the bowl underneath him as he gabbled out his praise, telling her she was perfect, the ideal woman, the ultimate Mistress. She merely laughed at him and continued to tug at his cock, until at last he was spent, when she reached out to tousle his hair.

'Good boy, that's right, that's what Mistress needs, and haven't you done a lot? Yes, you have, and you're going to eat it all up for me, aren't you?'

He responded with a sullen nod, desperate to please her and determined to obey her commands no matter what. It was exactly what he'd expected anyway, an old trick beloved of cruel women, to make a man come and then have him eat his own spunk immediately after he'd lost the full ecstasy of submission. David didn't even mind, despite the thick, salty taste as he poked his tongue out into the little pool of slimy white fluid. To serve his Mistress was what mattered, and if that meant eating his own spunk for her amusement, then it was a small price to pay.

She was smiling as she watched, and so was Madame Venus, both amused by his willingness to deliberately degrade himself. He was hoping they were both excited too, that maybe, just maybe, he would be permitted to serve them with his tongue, licking each to orgasm in turn. It didn't seem likely, as the only other time Madame

Venus had shared him with another woman they'd had their fun at his expense before locking him in the big iron cage with his chastity device on and his hands cuffed behind his back. They had gone upstairs to bed, together, leaving him to suffer the worst frustration of his life as he listened to the noises of their free, uninhibited passion from above. Yet Mistress Vixen was different, more independent and quite clearly in charge, while she'd not only bared her chest to add to his pleasure but left her big, beautiful breasts on show even when he was done. As he finished his revolting task she spoke again, her voice rich with delight and also excitement.

'Look, he's eaten it all up! Isn't he a good boy? What do you think, Venus, should I give him the reward I'm sure he wants?'

Madame Venus allowed herself a quiet smile.

'Make him beg for it. I always do. Although I don't always give him what he wants.'

David didn't need any further encouragement.

'Please, Mistress, I beg, humbly. I know I'm not worthy to touch you in any way at all, but I beg for the privilege of making you come, with my fingers, or if you'd grant me the ultimate privilege, with my mouth.'

Mistress Vixen reached out to stroke his hair.

'Cheeky little so-and-so, isn't he? So what, boy, do you want to give me oral sex, do you really want to, all the way?'

'Yes, Mistress. Please, Mistress. I beg to be allowed to serve you.'

'Hmm, yes, I can see you're keen, very keen. What a naughty boy you are.'

There was a curious inflection in Mistress Vixen's voice, but David ignored it, lost in bliss at the thought of being allowed to use his mouth on the beautiful dominatrix. He pulled himself to his knees, clasping his hands together in entreaty.

'Please, Mistress. Your humble slave begs to be permitted to serve you orally.'

Madame Venus began to use her whip to flick at his back and buttocks as Mistress Vixen stood up. David scarcely noticed, his mind fixed on what he was praying he'd be allowed to do, and it looked as if it was about to happen. Mistress Vixen had sat down, her legs well apart, and she'd begun to lift up her skirt. David could only stare as the rich black silk was tugged slowly up, to reveal her stockings tops and the soft, pale bulges of flesh where a few inches of her bare thighs showed. Her suspender straps came on show, and the front of a pair of lacy black panties, which she'd quickly pulled aside to expose not the neatly turned little cunt he'd been expecting, but a thick, heavy penis lying on a leathery scrotum. Madame Venus laughed.

'Be careful what you wish for, little boy, now get sucking, that is, if you ever want to see me again. Come on, David, in your mouth. I know you want to, so just fucking do it!'

David barely heard her words. He could only stare, fighting to resist the compulsion to take the horrible thing in his mouth, telling himself he wasn't gay, that he was no cock-sucker, that no man could possibly have made him feel the way he did as he was milked into the dog bowl, as he licked up his own spunk. But he'd done it, and he knew he couldn't resist what was being asked of him, not by his perfect Mistress, or maybe Master. He leant close. His mouth came wide. He hesitated for one last, awful moment, then for the first time in his life he took another man's cock into his mouth and begun to suck.

A Gift
Willow Sears

'You want to give *that* as a gift?'

'Well, it isn't any old birthday.' Sadie smiled. 'It is his fortieth after all.'

Rarely has someone been so appropriately named: Sadie the sadist. Still, I had to admit I liked her idea, a reaction made obvious by the wicked grin spreading across my face. And I suppose I felt honoured that she had come to me to execute her plan, although with my looks and reputation and with my Scold Room set up in my basement I was the obvious choice. I knew Sadie well enough, since you come to get acquainted with all your fellow Dommes on the scene, partly to share information and partly in a *keep your friends close and your enemies closer* kind of way. I had age on my side so I never considered her a major threat, although I could see why plenty did. Even in her everyday clothes and make-up she looked like a Domme.

She had sharp cheekbones and large, piercing eyes which bolstered her air of superiority. She was tall and worked out to maintain the muscle definition in her upper body, which she so liked to show off, despite her modest tits. But she couldn't prevent the weight she had chased from her top half seeking refuge in her bottom and thighs. Instead, she accentuated them, wearing the tightest skirts and trousers she could squeeze into, often donning strap-on toys over them so that the tight harness held her round cheeks even higher.

I felt a little nervy in her presence but you get that whenever you are face to face with one of your own kind. There is always a frisson between two Dommes, an unmentioned power struggle as if you are constantly sizing each other up and assessing whether a pre-emptive strike is necessary. Like two superpowers at a conference table it is all smiles and diplomacy, but in your head you are constantly thinking: *maybe I should just take this fucker out.* It's natural selection, you see. We need the Dommes as much as the Subs to create the scene, but each one potentially stands between you and what you want – namely a new victim to enslave and abuse. The best way to eliminate this threat is to master your adversary, either by driving them from the clubs you attend or defeating them physically and bringing them to heel. Once a Domme has been on the receiving end of humiliation or pain it is very hard for her to regain her former status and confidence.

The games we play are all about psychology and if you are ever shown to be weak, others will be reluctant to bow to any subsequent show of your strength. It rarely comes to bitch-fights on the club dance floors but many underhand methods have and will be used to bring rivals down a peg or two. There is a natural pecking order amongst all the Dommes and Masters, since that is only human nature, but for those of us at or near the top of this, there is greater reluctance to defer to anyone.

I quite liked Sadie, actually. For all her sternness I found her interesting and blessed with a cutting wit. It was hard to be too wary of someone casually lounging in jeans and a T-shirt and drinking a mug of tea.

'Shall I finger-fuck you?' I said.

It took her by surprise but she bit her lip and smiled and raised her eyebrows in an *ooo, that would be most lovely, you pussy-wettingly scrumptious young Goddess* expression.

She had a pleasingly hot cunt, doubtless warmed and lubricated through the simple excitement of being sat next to me. I wanked her fast and noisily and she closed her eyes and panted, not caring that she was at my mercy. I quickly took her all the way and she gave out a soft cry and squeezed my hand, pushing it into her as she creamed on my fingers. I took them out, smiled back at her, and wiped them across her lips; just a little show of my power over her.

'Now,' I said. 'You had better tell me exactly what you want me to do.'

Sadie was barely two years older than her brother. They had grown up in an isolated village and had by necessity been close, although with her naturally dominating character he had amounted to little more than her plaything. She loved him as you love any sibling and although she never wished him any harm, her impish nature often got him into trouble or saw him humiliated. The more she did it, the more he clung to her. She had a few friends from school close enough to see on occasions, but he had none. His dependency on her grew and he seemed incapable of making any decisions of his own accord, relying on her to run his life.

'He became a rather pathetic shadow,' she explained, 'although I have never felt anything other than absolute fondness for him.'

The quiet life was not for Sadie and so she moved away to London at the first opportunity, taking him with her. She knew he would be lost without her. They got a flat together and found work but she was propelled into the excitement of city life while he shrank from it. As he foundered they moved further apart and soon she set him adrift so that she could find herself. He spent his twenties silently getting by, working hard and keeping his head down. But a woman spotted him. The woman dragged him from his hidey-hole and made him her husband, although this amounted to being nothing more than her whipping boy. In a matter of years she was tired of him, citing his inability to sire a child as good reason to cast him out and take him for nearly everything he had. Sadie, also then single, came to the rescue and brought him back under her wing. Thus they had lived together in her large flat for the last few years. He doted on her as much now as he ever did, and she was way too proud not to love him for it.

'I am his only real love,' she said. 'It seems perverse, I know, but I am everything to him. He has had a crush on me for as long as I can remember and I'm afraid I can't help but use it to tease him mercilessly. I'm always cuddling him in a comforting, big sister kind of way, so he can smell my scent and feel my warmth all down his body, and the press of my tits against his chest. I sometimes let him glimpse me in my underwear. Other times, when I know he's pretending to be out, I masturbate loudly so he can listen at my bedroom door. It drives him madder each day to know that he cannot plunge his raging cock into his own flesh and blood, but I'm sure he wouldn't want me half as much if I wasn't his sister. It's the taboo element that makes him so frustrated and yet is so scintillating for him, so I play up to it, always getting too close and then reminding him of why we can go no further. My prick-teasing burns me with shame afterwards, but I'm simply addicted to his worship of me. Giving him this special gift is the best way I can think of to let him have something of me to treasure forever, something to make up for all the times I was mean to him. He will never know I gave it to him, but I will.'

What Sadie also meant, but didn't say, was that she would also get lots of kinky pleasure from having me do this for him. Always the sadist, it was of course as much or more about her as it was about him – a gift for them both. The plan was very simple: I would get her brother to come to my Scold Room as my slave. I would cover his head and tie him down, then tell him that my bitch was on her way over and that this bitch was in fact his sister. I would tell him I was going to trick her into fucking him. Sadie would indeed be there but her part would be played by another (one of my regular girls, Kitty, as it turned out). The apparently unwitting 'Sadie' would do her worst and then leave, none the wiser as to the identity of the wretched slave she had just abused. Then I would release him to go home and wank ever after to this cherished memory. A happy birthday indeed! I loved the idea and readily agreed, although me being me, I thought of a few little extras to spice up the proceedings.

* * *

The seduction, if you can call it that, was phenomenally easy, but then I never have any trouble in that department. I was informed that he went to the library late on Friday afternoons, so I tracked him there. I had to do little else except creep up on him and catch him unawares. When you are armed with the looks I've got, if you know what to say and how to say it, people like him are merely fish in a barrel.

'Your name is James, isn't it?' I said.

He stared at me, his face draining white with the shock of being addressed by a beautiful girl wearing a catsuit in skin-tight, black PVC. He barely managed to nod in affirmation of my question.

'It's a cuntish name,' I said. 'I think I will call you Arse Boy. You look like the kind of snivelling pervert who wants a dirty bitch to make him come. Do you want a good fucking, Arse Boy?'

Of course he did.

He probably would have gone with me just to stop my loud words attracting every single pair of eyes and ears towards us in our quiet surroundings. Just to be sure, I grabbed him by the wrist and pulled him away. I told him in the car that he was going to be my slave for the rest of the day and that if he was good then I would let him spunk at the end of it.

'I like good-for-nothing pieces of shit like you – they make me wet.'

It was only half-true, but I was pulling out all the stops to bag him and break him down as quickly as possible. I ordered him to take his cock out en route. He jumped at my words but managed to get his fumbling fingers to work and thus oblige me before I had to get nasty. Naturally, his prick was already erect, and it was a pretty good specimen – smooth and long and thin enough to be taken comfortably in any hole. I feigned my disdain, taking my eyes off the road just for a second to eject a mouthful of spit onto it. It hit the exposed tip and slid slowly down his twitching shaft to soak into his thick pubes.

* * *

I took him first to my basement kitchenette, adjoining the Scold Room. With Sadie already in position I needed him fully prepared before I brought him through. I had set up a lacy dressing screen for him to change behind, just to begin the theme of his emasculation. He swapped his clothes for the underwear I had put out: a bra, skimpy knickers and fishnet stockings, all in bright pink, all ludicrous against his hairy body. He was even given a pair of outsized pink high heels to set it off. I applied some garish glittery lipstick for him and then let him admire himself in the long mirror. Men are such suckers for this kind of thing. They look at it with dread but cannot help but love the feel of the nylon and soft cotton and lace against their skin, and the transformation it produces in them.

Sadie had sourced and paid for all the items – I was fucked if I was going to outlay anything when I was the one doing the favour! However, I had made his gimp mask myself, in pink rubber, with the words *Arse Boy* upon it in black. It had a small opening for his nose and a slightly larger one for his mouth, since suffocating him was never part of the original plan. Instead of eye holes there was a thick black zip running horizontally. Open, it would give a restricted, slitty view of the world. Closed, it would leave him completely blind.

I sat him in the straight-backed chair that I had brought in from the Scold Room. It is in black iron with a pointed arch top-rail, with shackles at either side where the back meets the seat for you to secure the wrists of your victim (all very gothic). I have a set of them which I use during dinner parties, interspersing selected naked slaves amongst my invited guests to be fondled or spattered with food and drink. You can even climb on the table and piss on them if the mood takes you. He allowed me to shackle him without resistance, but I could feel his whole body trembling. Then I showed him the gimp mask.

'This is a very tight fit,' I said, 'perhaps too tight. I think I am going to have to shave your head.'

He started to wriggle but it was already way too late for that. I set up a smaller mirror on the table so that he could watch it all. I took off the bulk of his locks with the hair clippers, shearing him as close to the skin as I could. Then I lathered him up and carefully removed the remnants, completely exposing his pale scalp. His face was set in horrified surprise but his cock was like a bar in his knickers and the tip of it was stretching the fabric of the waistline and peeking out, crying a tear of pre-come. I towelled off his egg-head and let him see it in all its glory.

'How are you going to explain this to your sister?' I said. It was the first time I had mentioned Sadie at all, or given any indication that I knew of her. His eyes widened still further at the sound of her name and he started to speak, but a sharp slap to the face cut him dead.

'You don't say a fucking word until I tell you, Arse Boy,' I snarled, 'not even when I bend you over. Not even when your backside is being used.'

I wanted him to be in no doubt, right from the start, that his rectum was going to be filled. I poured olive oil straight from the bottle onto his shining crown and smoothed it into the skin. This allowed the mask to be pulled over his head with less of a struggle, although it was still several minutes before it was properly in place. I allowed him a brief look through the eye slit at his reflection, letting him witness his glittery pink lips protruding grotesquely through their tight opening. Then I zipped him shut. His prick did not seem to mind that the pitiful specimen it was attached to was now blind. If anything it seemed even more excited, poking out further for attention. I fastened a dog lead to the ring at the bottom of the mask. I then released his hands and led him inside the Scold Room, casting Sadie a little wink as I passed her. I bent him over one of the Fuck Benches and secured his wrists once more, then pulled down his little pink knickers to expose his arse. He didn't give me any trouble at all.

The bench was a padded frame supporting him under his thighs and upper torso, but with a gap to allow his cock and balls to hang free. I wheeled over the drip-stand with the bag already filled with clear lubricating oil. I put the tube to his anus and released the valve but shut it again quickly so that only a quick gush hit his hole. He was undoubtedly very new to all this so I thought it best to break him in gently. I selected a long thin butt plug and pressed it to his anus.

'Any minute now your sister is going to come through that door,' I said. 'She won't know who you are but I will tell her you are a worthless spunk-guzzler who needs his disgusting arse stretched wide open and fucked.'

The words made him whimper and this escalated to a long grunting sigh as I thrust the plug up inside him. As he lay panting, I turned to witness Sadie's reaction. Her cheeks were flushed and her eyes were wide, possibly even showing trepidation at what I was planning. She couldn't speak out, of course, so I just smiled at her and blew her a kiss. I next turned to Kitty, sat in the other corner obediently awaiting her cue. I signalled for her to move and she went over to the door, opening it as if she had just made her entrance.

'Ah Sadie, there you are,' I said theatrically.

He audibly drew in his breath and I saw his buttocks clench, his rectum squeezing on the toy inside him in either apprehension or anticipation. I flashed another knowing smile at the real Sadie before addressing her.

'I said I would reward you for licking my bum so well, and here is your prize!'

He let go another gasp at the words, perhaps with the mental image of his sister on her back and my rump spread across her face. It was fun taking advantage of her current position and having her sound like nothing more than an arse slave, so I gave her another big smile and a cheeky wink. I told 'Sadie' to strip and had her tie off his cock and balls with her stocking. I made sure the inexperienced Kitty did it right, winding the material around each nut individually so that they bulged against the scrotum, then winding it around the base of his prick and tying it tight. I don't think the harridan who once purported to be his loving wife could have ever treated my poor victim to anything like this, not judging by the bubbling squeals he was now emitting. With his cock tied, I felt he was ready and it wouldn't go off too soon, despite his obvious excitement. I needed him to keep his climax in check for later. I had promised him he would get to spunk and I wasn't lying.

I decreed that before anything else, he had to be filled up. I slid the plug from his butt and tossed it onto his back, making him shiver at the slimy touch on his skin. This time I fed the tube up into his rectum before releasing the valve. He immediately jerked and yelped as the fluid flowed into him. He was panicking but I told him to hang on and try to relax, to take as much as he could and hold it, since it would make his fucking so much easier to bear. He was whimpering again and I thought it best to calm him down or his arse would be harder to open than a tortoise. 'Bitch, let him smell your cunt and bum.'

I saw him tremble once more, perhaps through the incredulity of me calling his beloved sister such a name, as well as the promise of what she was about to do. 'Sadie' did as instructed in her role, going around the front of the bench and bending over in his face, holding his head between her open cheeks and writhing as he tried to catch the scent of her holes through the small opening for his nostrils. I noticed his prick jerking beneath him and wondered if it was through the oil pressing on the gland inside him or because her pussy or shit-hole had tantalisingly opened up against his nose and left the tip wet. I called her off and told her to come back around and remove the tube from inside him, since I didn't want any of his dirty release spurting out onto *me*. However, he did well and held it all, his anus twitching as the muscles fought back the flood. I picked a cat-o'-nineteen tails from the wall. It was short handled and you could give it a good rip through the air. It would hurt but the many tresses tended to spread and dampen the impact. I handed it to my girl and instructed her to deliver the strokes. Sure enough he yelped again, but it was more through shock than pain and his cock was visibly swelling around the nylon restraining it. She lashed him more, sending out a series of blows across his back, legs and buttocks. None of them even coloured his skin. I handed her a cane instead, giving her strict instructions on how to lay down each fiery stroke. This definitely hurt him, right from the first contact. If his pain hadn't been tempered by the erroneous belief that it was his sister dealing out the beating, I'm sure he would have screamed. It wasn't that hard but each was a cutting impact, a real blow of searing intensity that made his buttocks clench together and jangled his nerves. Then, as he waited for the next blow, the endorphin rush would sweep him and you could see the tremors all through his body. After the fifth stroke he couldn't contain himself any longer, and spurted out maybe half of the oil cramping his arse before he was able to regain control and hold it in.

This signalled time for the main event. I squirted cold lotion across his buttocks to give them some relief. I next took up the dildo I had picked especially for his deflowering, locating it within the harness that Kitty was to wear. Sadie the sadist looked a little shocked at the length of the dildo and even shook her head a fraction. But it had to be that long, or the word ARSEFUCKER would never have fitted along its length in the large letters raised up from the otherwise smooth, hard shaft. I made little ceremony of the penetration, merely calling Kitty 'Sadie' a couple more times as she was preparing, to reinforce the pretence that I was curtly ordering his own sister to strap on the dildo and drive it home past all his resistance. Again it would have hurt but it would also be the most exhilarating, blissful feeling he would ever have, especially as he thought his most coveted dreams were at last coming true. The oil leached out of him on her every back stroke and then she forced herself forward again, driving even further as his muscles relented. I made her fuck him hard and deep, the dildo prodding ever forward towards his sensitive gland.

I went over to the real Sadie, still silent but breathless as she watched her birthday present being given such an ecstatic reception. I smiled and kissed her on the cheek, grabbing her hair and pulling it a little to bring her face properly into contact with my lips. I saw her hands clench and unclench in anguish but she had to stay quiet. I went behind her and pulled her knickers down to her knees, prising open her fat bum cheeks and spitting on her little hole. I worked two fingers up inside her, just to give her a little taste of the joy her brother was feeling because of her kindness.

Kitty thrust away, hammering the toy in and out of him amidst the noisy squelches from his oily arse. When she was fully inside him I had her lie forward so that she was resting her bare chest against his back, cuddling him as she humped him like a dog. I left Sadie's rear end and came back around in front of her. I pulled up my skirt and pressed my bare bottom into her face. I could feel her saliva on me and the hardness of the plastic ball pressing to my so-tight quim. I shoved my hand down between my thighs and rubbed my clit, my orgasm coming almost instantly as I watched him being fucked.

When I could speak again I ordered Kitty to dismount. She was spent anyway and just lying against him, the dildo filling his arse. As quietly as I could, I led her over to the open door and signalled for her to leave.

'Right, bitch,' I said, as if 'Sadie' were still present. 'Get on your knees down here.'

I clanked a bit of nearby equipment for effect and smirked at the real Sadie, who would obviously know what I was trying to make him believe was happening. I then untied him and peeled him off the bench to release his prick from the stocking at last. He followed on shaking legs as I took him over and behind his sister.

'My bitch fucked you as a reward for giving me a good licking, but I also know she is a dirty cunt who has been fucking all sorts of people behind my back, in the most disgusting ways you can imagine.'

I opened the zip across his eyes just briefly, just to give him a glimpse of her on all fours before him. He would see her wiggling fat arse and know it was plump enough to be hers. And just before I zipped him up again, I pulled her head up so that he would see her hair and know it was the right colour.

'She needs to be punished and since she has just fucked you I see no reason why you shouldn't give her exactly the same back. I am going to let you have her. You may fuck her any way you like.'

Poor Sadie. She bucked and squealed but what she had planned as a harmless pervy game was about to backfire in spectacular fashion. Her fate was close to being sealed. Honestly, I cannot believe I got her into the stocks so easily – it was laughable really. All I did was tell her to copy me and give it a go so she could feel how the padding under the neck just slightly choked you. She bloody did it! She got down on her knees, even put her hands where they were meant to rest and all I had to do was close the thing over her! I still don't think she understood the full implication and I'm sure she wouldn't have let on even, once her brother was in the room, but I put the ball-gag on her anyway. Shame really – I would like her to have licked my arse while I came. Still, she is mine now if I choose so there could be plenty of that later.

His trembling hands moved forward and found her thighs and ever so slowly he moved forward so that his prick was between her cheeks, ready to give her the rough, deep fuck of his dreams. As far as he knew, she did not know who he was, so as long as he kept the mask on, his identity would not be revealed to her. He was on the threshold of having the miracle he dreamt of and as far he was concerned, she would never know. I could let him take what he wanted or I could drag him off and agonizingly rob him of his one big chance. It all depended on who I thought deserved my cruelty most. I had one last chance to stop him, to call him off before things went too far …

* * *

I don't hate Sadie, I quite like her really, but my pervy side is always in so much danger of getting the better of me. If I don't stop him right now then she will stop being my friend and start being merely my slave. I will know her dirty secret so there will be nothing she can do except anything and everything that I tell her. Her one hope would be that he never discovered that she knew what happened. I shouldn't put her through this but the thought exhilarates me and she had such a nice juicy cunt when I fingered her on my sofa, and that is something I can never get enough of. I'm still in two minds. I will lose a companion who makes me laugh, and I have precious few of those. Plus it would be one of *the* meanest things I have ever done to anyone, let alone a supposed friend. But it is an opportunity I surely cannot overlook. Sadie is a Domme, so she will understand how difficult it is for me to stop myself. I just cannot resist breaking bitches and bringing them under my control, whoever they are and whatever they mean to me. I find it all so overwhelmingly sexy, perhaps more so because I am just so damn good at it. My talents are, let's face it, a gift.

Chameleon
Lara Lancey

Normally a man like this one would consider himself way out of my league. We wouldn't even cross paths, at least not socially, let alone have a conversation or the chance to get up close and personal. Oh, I've met his type in a professional capacity plenty of times, but superior people like him walk around with their heads up in the clouds. Way up their arses, more like. He would never remember someone like me.

Not unless we'd fucked, in which case he would never, ever forget.

No, I'm not a hooker by the way, despite the temptations. Some of my best friends are hookers. But being dynamite in the sack is just one of my special skills. It's not the way I make my living, though you'd be amazed at how many men, and a quite a few women, have asked over the years, begged even, to fuck me, and when I've tossed my pretty head and pretended to be affronted at the idea, they've offered me money for the privilege.

Have I taken the money? You betcha.

But I won't put out for any old bit of rough. My friends say I'm always punching above my weight. They say rough is all I'm good for. But after years of slumming it I've become every bit as good as the smart guys I con. I may not have started out that way, but I've gotten through life by becoming a prize chameleon. My victims would never know the difference.

So, I like them upmarket. Successful. Important. Super respectable. Pillars of society – the more upstanding the pillar the better. There was that priest, who looked after me when I used to pop into his church and sit in the confessionals to keep warm. That doctor, who took me under his white coat when he found me in the geriatric ward weeping by the bedside of a random old lady. That French businessman who paid for my ticket and a whole lot besides when I decided to, how shall I put it, take a trip on Eurostar to get away from it all.

'You've the face of an angel and a devil's body.' That's what the Irish priest said, barely able to breathe after I'd finished with him. Actually, mate, it's the other way round, if you only knew.

I suppose you could say I have a thing for uniforms. Anyone in uniform's going to be the opposite of me, let's face it, although I run into them more than most. And it's a challenge, isn't it, formal dress. A kind of shield. Father Mike was sexy enough, in a grey-haired kind of way, once I'd got him out of all those girly vestments. I couldn't shag someone ugly. I do have some standards. So it seemed only fair after he'd taken me into the presbytery, put me up and fed me, to show his poor neglected cock how good it would feel ramming up inside a woman for the first time.

But all that was a while ago. I've been otherwise engaged for some time now, so I'm up for some action today and this guy I'm looking at now? Well, I'd pay him if I had the dosh. The black gown, flapping round him like some kind of vampire's cloak. The stiff collar and white tie. He's holding the old horsehair under his arm and I have to say those wigs make even the plainest of men look distinguished. But this one's gorgeous, especially if, like me, you're into the authority vibe. If you're the sort who fancied your teacher, say, or your dad's best friend. If you like bringing them to their knees.

And what do you know? We're standing side by side, the only two people in a very small lift. He's probably the most senior person I've come across in the legal chain. Barring an actual judge, of course.

'Going up?' he asks, long finger hovering over the button.

I look right at him. His eyes are green. I've never been very good at looking people in the eye, except when I'm lying. So I decide to look straight at his crotch.

'I'd rather go down.'

He has a wide mouth, pulling up in a big smile. Front teeth white, slightly crooked. He puts his hand up in a fist to his mouth and coughs. 'Right. I take it you mean you're in a hurry to go to the cells.'

He's got the way my mind works. He may be decent, like all the others, clean leaving, law abiding, but they're all the same under their zippers, aren't they? They all have the same urges, easily roused. They all have the same cocks, ready to get stiff at the slightest hint or joke or touch.

'Sorry. Smutty joke. I must be nervous.' I give a lady-like little shiver. 'I can't bear it down there, even after all this time. I mean, it's the dark side, isn't it? They make it deliberately grim. Those smelly rooms, the way the doors clang shut. Those caged men with their dead eyes. The awful things they've done.'

'And that's just the barristers!'

I laugh, and my stomach goes tight. Oh, he's good, this one. He'll do very nicely. 'I'm always afraid one of them will pounce on me, take me hostage or something.'

'The criminals or the barristers?' He laughs again, and then, as always happens when a conversation has started up, his face goes serious. He strokes his chin to hide it. 'I can think of one or two who would jump at the chance of taking you hostage.'

His hand is tanned against the snow-white cuff of his

shirt. It's winter, so a rich man like him has probably been wintering in the Caribbean or skiing somewhere. There are golden hairs streaking his wrist. No wedding ring.

'Well, either way I've changed my mind. I think I'll take the ground floor, please.' I tap the file in my arms and brush an imaginary speck off my tight grey jacket. 'My junior can go and see the client. I've had enough of the Crown Court for one day.'

He nods and presses the button. The lift jolts, then stops. It could be the control room, waking up to the situation and forcing an emergency stop, blocking all exits from the building. But I still have time on my side.

'I don't suppose you could help me out with something before you run away?' His voice has gone deeper.

I slide out of the eyeshot of the wall-mounted camera and take a good look at him. My eyes are busy tracking up his long legs, lingering on the zip securing his smart, striped trousers. I've got this habit from hours of hanging around in police stations. You manage the situation by picturing what's in men's pants. Not the crims. Their cocks are always hard, always dirty. It's those in uniform, as I told you, who I get off on. The most brutish sergeant becomes a sex dog if you just get an image of what his stiff cock looks like. How big. What it could do to you, if only you'd let him. How grateful he'd be.

The man in this lift has a flat stomach under that crisp, white shirt. He'll be tanned from his holidays, a trail of dark hair like an arrow directing me to that fan of hair and the quiet beast resting against his thigh. If I carry on looking he'll sense it, even though I'm being very polite, and the beast will start to lift away from his leg, getting hard. When I get the nerve I'll just reach out for a little touch, see it stiffen and push against his trousers.

The lift jolts again, banging me against the wall. I raise my eyes. He's looking right back at me. He's noticed this natty grey suit I'm wearing. It's much too tight. My tits are busting out of it, but I thought buttoned up looked better. And if that gun in his pocket means he's pleased to see me, then he thinks so too.

'I was going to suggest the exact same thing,' I say, as an idea occurs to me. 'You look like you're struggling under all those files. Do you need a hand taking your briefs back to your, you know …'

There it goes. The first button pops off the jacket. I've only got a tiny petticoat on underneath, and again, it's much too small. My poor solicitor Janette is still locked up in the ladies' loo, hands and feet bound with pink tape, her teeth jammed onto my socks so she can't yell out. I didn't have time to dress her up in my jeans and sweatshirt, so whoever finds her will have a treat, because she's a cute little thing and half-naked, sprawled on the cold tiled floor in her very expensive white underwear and nothing else. She must be a couple of sizes smaller than me, but I needed her clothes to look the part.

'… Chambers?' He really is into me, but then he's red-blooded like any other male. My breasts are bulging over the top of the pink petticoat, pushing through the jacket, and as he takes the wig and jams it onto his head he can't help running his eyes over me. It makes my nipples tingle.

'Actually,' he says, 'I was hoping that you'd be able to sit behind me in court for one last hearing. My pupils's gone home. Then perhaps we could run away together? At least to the nearest restaurant!'

The lift jerks and starts scraping upwards, away from the ground floor and the outside world, away from the only exit. I won't panic. In fact, let's consider the running away with him idea. It could be exactly the cover I need, if I can just avoid the CCTV and persuade him to take me out the back way. My cunt twitches with excitement, as if I need to piss. I always get like this if I'm in a spot of bother. I'm so excited now we wouldn't get further than the alleyway behind the court house before I'd have to shove him against the wall and lift my skirt – or rather, Janette's silly skirt – for him. Oh, yes. Lust like this has got me into trouble before.

'I can't help you, I'm afraid. I really have to leave right now.' I fuss about, tugging my jacket closed. I let my fingers linger, twiddling the single button hanging by a thread. He looks at it too. I struggle to fasten it, pulling myself about, squeezing my breasts together making a nice deep cleavage.

'Like, I'm a criminal, get me out of here?'

I laugh softly. If only he knew. I bite the end of my finger. Something about the warm, wet swirl of my own tongue on my skin gets me going, and now he's looking at my finger I start to suck on it. Then I smile, pulling the finger out with a pop. 'There's a getaway car waiting for me, and everything.'

The lift dings as we approach the top floor. He opens his mouth to say something, and just then the second button snaps right off my jacket and skitters across the dirty lino. When I bend over to try to find the button my breasts tumble forward and right out of the petticoat. They're a shock to behold, all plump and pale in the harsh strip light.

'Let me help.' He bends as well, totally unnecessary, but he bumps me so I topple onto my knees. The jacket slips down my arms. Now I really am on a level with his crotch, a couple of inches away. I can feel the heat beating off him, see the thick shape growing bigger in his trousers. He straightens again and closes his eyes. The twin tails of his wig jiggle with the pulse in his neck.

I think fast, as I'm used to doing all the time. I can't stop this now it's started. I want this guy, and he wants me. It takes over me, this lust, it takes me right to the edge. I have to weigh it up, work it out. Make a decision. My body, pulsing with lust now, takes over.

'Kill the lift,' I say quietly as the doors start to open.

He jabs the red button with his elbow, eyes still shut, and we're prisoners again. I can see him swallowing.

I unzip him, get my hand inside his flies, pause to see if he'll stop me, then as soon as I touch his cock I'm horny as hell, and obviously so is he. He gasps, and that flicks the switch for me. I love a man at my mercy. I bury my head in his lap, smell the sweat and the hint of spunk and now his penis is jumping into my face. I lick the tip like it's my lollipop. It jumps again and he pulls back but only for a second, totally losing control as he shoves himself back at me. His knob slips stickily into my mouth.

I allow myself a smirk. How many of those skinny solicitors go down on their men like this? And how often does it happen in the lift at work? I follow the motion of his body with my mouth so as not to lose him.

He can't even touch me. He's still holding all those files. I grip the top of his legs and keep the moist tip of his cock firmly in my mouth. His cock presses against my tongue, rubs against my teeth. I open my jaw wider. He's huge now. I push the rigid shaft away from my throat with my tongue. Every move makes him stiffer. I start to suck and I can taste him, clean skin mixed with the sweet salt trickling through the slit. He starts to groan and thrust against the roof of my mouth. I love it. My tongue traces the veins on its surface. My mouth moves up and down and I nip the taut flesh. He pushes in really roughly, spreading his thighs further to get a better angle, and his buttocks start to buck at me.

He's going to shoot his load any minute, and what's the point in that? I'm too good at this, that's my problem. There's barely any time until the lift starts up again, or the doors open, and I'm not leaving here until I've had some. I want him to fuck me, and fast. In a couple of minutes we'll be caught.

He's thinking the same, because he drags himself out of my mouth, drops his bundle of files, and thumps after them to the floor. He pulls me down on top of him so that I am straddling his crotch, hitching my nicked skirt up round my bottom and literally ripping off my knickers. This is so much better than shagging one of the lads from the old days, dragging some dreg out of the pub and into the rain so we can get to it before closing time. What's so much hornier about this scenario, apart from the very real danger of it all, is getting a posh bloke like this down and dirty, grunting like an animal, ripping at my bra so he can grab my tits, squeezing them and shoving his face in between them, tweaking and biting at my nipples till it hurts.

It makes me squeal, makes me open my pussy lips to rub against the length of his cock as he sucks till it hurts. I'm so hot now. I get hold of his prick, kneel up so that the tip, still wet from my tongue, noses into my crack then I lean forward so my tits crush him and he bites and sucks even harder.

I rock slightly on my knees, letting his knob tease my burning clit, no further inside, just tickle the surface, prepare me, use him like a toy before I lower myself onto him, down that long, thick shaft. The smooth surface is lovely and slippery where I've slicked it with my saliva and my honey.

My posh barrister's head crashes back against the metal wall of the lift, his collar tight around his Adam's apple, his mouth opening to pant and groan, his big hands warm on my bare thighs.

Voices are shouting somewhere in the building and the lift seems to sway. Clock's ticking. I grind down hard on him now, no more messing, sliding right down. His cock rubs my burning clit and then it's fitting hard inside me, impaling me so that I could spin on it.

I'm licking my lips as I start the stroke up and down, his cock still getting bigger and harder, then every inch of him grazing every screaming inch of me so that I can only go so far before slamming back down on him and each time I do his knob is hard as rock.

'What's the rush?' He grabs my hips to slow me down. 'You'll go at my pace, young lady. They won't start the hearing without me. With any luck they'll adjourn it.'

But I'm the one in control, not him. I give a couple of strong tight squeezes on his cock with my cunt and it's like a kind of electric shock on him because he jerks wildly and then he's the one slamming it up inside me as

I ride down to meet him. He's really lost it and we bang against each other and he gets harder, I get wetter, flames streak through me, my tits bounce as I grind about on top of him. When his eyes start to glaze over that does it and I need to be quick and I start to come, up here on the top floor, shagging some QC knob in a grimy lift. I think he's going to keep this going for hours but then he shouts out like a schoolboy as his cock bucks and his spunk pumps into me, throwing me upwards with the strength of his climax.

The voices are nearer now. My legs are aching from being spread so wide over him but I clamber off him, my skirt rucked up over my fanny, juice tangling my pubes, nipples still burning red as I pull up the little petticoat and yank down my skirt over my bare snatch. He packs away his lovely, well-bred cock – what a waste – and zips up his trousers just as the lift plummets down again to the ground floor and the doors slide open.

We fall out into the waiting area. It smells of stale smoke, sweat, and sins. The first person I see at the far end is my solicitor Janette, weeping and wailing and looking awful wearing my baggy old jeans and sweater. She's obviously ready to kill me.

'You still haven't told me who you are,' the barrister hisses, grabbing my shoulder as everyone starts to crowd round. 'Where are your chambers? I could call you.'

I have to laugh. 'I'm not a barrister, love. Not any

kind of lawyer. But you can come and visit my chamber any time. When I know which wing it's on –'

'You're a prison officer?'

I shake my head. They're screaming a name over the Tannoy. Angela, that's what I've told them, after the sweet things the priest said about my face.

'Try prisoner.'

Heavy feet are running towards us. Guns and cuffs jangling against body armour. Oh, why didn't I leg it when I had the chance? I could have taken my sexy new friend with me.

'What's the charge?' he demands to know, taking hold of my arm.

'Caught red-handed with my hands in the till.' I step out of the lift and stand legs apart, hands on hips, waiting.

He still doesn't get it, not even when the coppers burst along the thin carpet, ready to tackle me to the floor. I recognise one of them. He's overweight and puffing as he comes up to me.

'See you've dyed your hair and changed your image, Angela. Didn't recognise you. Not even on the CCTV.'

His new sidekick has barely started shaving. He'll do nicely. His buttocks are high and pert in his thick trousers. This one hooks my arm up behind my back, and of course the tight jacket starts to slip off again, and my tits fall right out for everyone to see.

'Why do they need the bloody cavalry to take you

for a fraud offence?' The barrister bellows as they click shut the handcuffs. 'Who the hell was your employer?'

'God was her employer, mate.' The officers laugh at that as they march me between them towards the door. 'And that poor old Father Michael.'

There's a rush of fresh air from outside. I start to struggle as hard as I can, all leg-kicking, pussy-flashing, seam-splitting. May as well give them all an eyeful. Janette's suit is in tatters now.

'But a priest wouldn't have much to steal.' My knight in shining armour. He's not giving up. He's stamping along behind us as they drag me towards the wagon waiting in the car port.

'Try a hundred grand from the church fund, sir. All those Sunday collections. Angela here is truly wicked.' The young copper's done his homework, I'll give him that. 'Then she went on the run, didn't she, kept changing her identity, and blew the lot. It's taken us and Interpol months to track her down for this offence and a load of others and we're not letting her get away again.'

The barrister tries one last time with his best court-room voice. 'But surely you can stop manhandling her like that, officer! She's hardly dangerous is she?'

Everyone laughs raucously at that. Even me. I feel a little sorry for him, but you see, it's he who is way out of my league when it comes to danger. I mean, he has no idea how handy I am with gaffer tape and a sawn-off.

'You've been had by this one, sir. Every which way.' The younger copper sniggers as fat cop unlocks the back door of the wagon. 'CCTV showed us everything!'

'Shut it, officer.' I punch him with my elbow, forcing him to grab me tighter. 'You'll see. Father Mike deserved it. They all deserved it!'

'Save it for the judge,' says my young cop.

'You've been watching too many movies, mate,' I snort, going limp in his arms. 'And you have no idea what I'm saving for the judge!'

The cop marches me up the steps of the van. I can tell from the way he's pressed up behind me that he's well hung. I wriggle against his hard-on, the skirt riding up hopelessly around my bare bum. I hope he can smell the sex on me as I lift one leg to step up. That was my last shag as a free woman, perhaps, but this is just the beginning.

Where I'm going they're a butch bunch by all accounts, and obviously all female. I'll have this cop before the day's out, right here in the prison van if need be. And then I guess I'll get the taste for a screw. I mean, what else am I going to do inside?

Land of Pleasure
Kim Mitchell

Here I am, *in medias res* as they say, sitting in my car, parked half a block from your house. Watch your guests arrive, all these women, beautiful women. The bridal shower, that necessary ritual for the-about-to-get-married. Try to calm myself. Know this is hopeless. The night so long dreamed and hoped for has finally arrived. My arrival: a surprise for *you*, ma'am. Heart pounding, unsure of your reaction and my ability to dampen and conceal my desire for you.

Inner voice: *'Just say hello. Act normal. Smile at everyone. No one will know. Maybe a touch will pass between us. Casual, as you greet all your friends. Don't stay long. Perhaps a whispered endearment. Then go.'* Yes, I can do this. Open the car door. Sounds from the house muted, my footsteps crushing the gravel. *Crunch, crunch, crunch.* The sounds make me think of eating your pussy. That is funny. Why? I hold in a laugh.

Another guest has arrived and follows me up the walk. I turn and smile and she smiles back: we both belong here. We both crunch the gravel.

Door opens and I'm met by a smiling woman. She looks at me, realizes we've never met before, welcomes me in, along with Penny or Paula, whatever her name is, the woman behind me. I'm inside and she's taking my coat. Clasp the bottle tightly and keep it. Want to give it to you, no one else, so *you* know it came from *me*.

Women talking. Feel their eyes on me. Before they can ask questions, I hear your voice:

'Yo, Penny, and who is this fine ...?'

Our eyes meet and I see the fire of emotions in your pupils. The shock on your face, replaced at once with the most wonderful smile I remember so well.

'*Kelly?* Kelly, is it really *you*? I wasn't expecting *you*!'

Tongue: glued to the roof of my mouth.

You take my hand, fingers tight and I squeeze. Relieved, delirious that you are welcoming me and so delighted to see me. You're talking to the women but I don't hear the words, lost in my gaze: your body, your hair, your mouth.

See your eyes move down and your spell over me is broken. I lift up the bottle and present it to you. Your favourite, Cabernet: 2001.

Voice thick and husky, 'Lauren, you're so beautiful, you're ...'

Don't finish.

You pull my body toward your body. Hand sweaty as you take me through the crowd. Women turn as we pass, looks and inquiries ignored as we move through their bodies. Faces a blur, one or two catch for a second. Long enough for them to register. So many guests and yet we ignore them all. Or, you ignore them. I'm oblivious in your wake.

We reach the stairs; you lead me up; at the top, you stop and we turn to look back. Some have taken little notice of our destination; others *stare and know.*

You take me from room to room, displaying me.

I am so proud standing at your side, hands locked. Hot courses of electricity dancing in my body; from head to toe but concentrated in my loins, liquid and hot, failing to contain it.

You say, 'They now *see* that my bitch is *here.* See how jealous they are of me! Of my gift, that you are and that I will take now.'

You pull me again. In a rush we are in your bedroom and I am in your arms. I kiss you with a hunger I cannot give words to. I know your equal desire too well. You press me up against the closed door, crushing me in your need. Your lips so much more luscious; mouth sweeter than I remembered.

Hook a leg around yours. Bare legs touching. Sucking on your tongue, I feel you lift me and carry me across to your bed. You lay me down and stand back to look at me. Now given a chance, I gaze and take you in. Seeing your fingers working, removing clothes.

'What are you waiting for?' you say, and command: 'Get undressed! I will whip you later for surprising me like this. *First I need to fuck.* Even though they will all know ... because they *will all know* ... my *need* to *fuck* you can't be withheld.'

My shoes hit the floor before you finish and my top is over my head a moment later. I had risked no undies and now glad I did this. Tear at the clasp and zipper on my skirt, working it off my hips half-undone. Pull down the comforter and covers, knowing they will be ruined otherwise. Now on the soft coolness of your sheets, I await.

You: on the bed, kneeling before me. I know what you want and I sit up and kiss your belly. Arms around waist. Touch and taste being the foremost, but also listening to you tell me that *I better be a good slut and please you.* Seeing with unbelieving eyes that you have me in your bed. Smelling your pussy, knowing that soon I will be enjoying it.

Tongue traces through your curly short pubes. Wetting them with my saliva so that they clump together. My mouth finds your clit. Taking hold, sucking it. Hands holding your ass so I can suck properly. You don't wait. Hands gripping my head. Your hips move. Fucking my mouth with it. Motions hard, almost violent.

'Come on, bitch! You can do better than that!'
If not for your hands holding me, I would have been
knocked flat on my back from the force of your thrusts.
Clit moving between my lips. I use my lips to assist you,
tight but not too tight. You can move it in between them
and I feel it increasing your lust. My tongue lashes at
the tip each time you drive forward.

You: a handful of hair in your fist and yank my head
back. Your knees spread and straddling me. You force
my face into your pussy. Grinding hard on me as I try
to get my tongue into you. I can *taste you* but it's more
from your wetting my entire face than from my tongue
being able to pleasure you. Once again hands at the
back of my head holding me as you rub up and down,
back and forth.

A pause in your actions that allows me to work my
tongue in. Savouring the taste of your pussy, my life
complete now that my mouth is full of your juice.

Your fingers weaving through my hair, soothing, gentle.
You pull back from me and slide down beside me. We
share a kiss. I wonder at your change, knowing that your
orgasms were small, not complete.

You leave me and return with two glasses of wine. I
see the bottle: the winery, Cabernet, 2001 ... *my bottle*
... now opened and poured.

Toast and sip. Your eyes telling me that you're far
from done with me. You take the glass from my hand

and place it on the nightstand. Another long, deep kiss. Then another, and another. I could kiss you for ever and this alone fills that empty thing inside.

A long finger inside me. Gasping into your mouth. You finger-fuck my pussy. Hips moving with it. *The touch magic.* The pressure of the base of your fingers on my clit and I try to rub on you.

'My baby bitch needs fucking, doesn't she?'

'Please, ma'am, whatever you desire,' is my answer.

'You'll be *made* all right. I will fuck you until you pass out in my arms.'

Whimper, holding you tight. Groaning, feel your hand and finger leave me.

You roll on me, our legs entwined. Taking a leg, you lift it up and use it to settle yourself. Our pussies kissing, wetness combining, mingling. You hold my leg between your breasts and use it for leverage. Grinding down. Push my hips up. Giving my pussy to you, always you. And you're inside me. My wetness allowing you easy and ready access. Your clit moves along my pussy lips, thrusts in like a cock.

'That's what I like to hear,' you say. 'My fuck toy makes such lovely sounds. Tell me you love to be fucked.'

Know the words you like to hear: 'Please fuck me, ma'am. I love how you fuck me. I'm your whore. *Your fucking whore*. YOUR BITCH!'

Grasp your hips and leg. Here's my pussy, giving it to

you to fuck. Wanting, *needing* you to fuck it. One arm remains wrapped around my leg, holding it tight to your chest. The other reaches out and rips at my hair.

'You *are* my bitch! And I will bitch fuck you! And beat you! And piss on you! Then bitch fuck you again!'

The bed: protesting under us.

I cry out again, the wet heat of your love along with the rapid continued pounding of your pussy with mine having again brought me to orgasm. Only the tug of your hand at my hair keeps me from falling.

You release me. Eyes opening to see you rise up and bending over to kiss me softly.

'Stay here. I'll be back after my guests leave. Then I will *really* fuck you and not hold back.'

Curling up in your bed sheets. Listen to the sounds of the wedding shower party wind down. Can hear your laughter and voice.

Eyes closed. Sleep. Happy.

* * *

Wake in the dark to new sounds. The bed shaking. My eyes rapidly adjusting to the dim light, I make out soft moans and grunts, bits of conversation. *The sound of fucking.*

See you at the foot of the bed. Hands on the foot-board, bracing. Behind you, I make out another form. Don? Both of you are looking at me.

'This is so *hot*.'

'Want to fuck her?'

'She's awake.'

'Yes, she is. And she sees us now. Sees you fucking *me*.'

I can't take my eyes off *you* with *him*.

'She's young.'

'Yes, she is. In her twenties. Loves to fuck.'

The rhythmic slap of flesh on flesh.

'Are you …?'

'Yeah.'

'Remember what I told you!'

'I do, ma'am.'

A rush: he moves away from your body. I can make out the shape of his cock in his hand as his body makes its way to my body. Thick and clutched in his fist. A shaft of moonlight catches him just as he stands next to me. I can see it. *Red, wet, throbbing,* all those things you call a cock.

The first rope of his semen shoots out and hits me square across the face: raised line from right cheek, across my lips and down my chin. The trailing end falls on my neck and left breast. Another follows and, knowing you are looking, *expecting,* I open my mouth for it. It is another long strand; salty goo fills my mouth. A third spurt, less volume, lands on my breasts. His hand pumping the last out, smaller, thinner spurts. Drops. Dew drops of baby batter. Some reaches me; some only finds the bed.

I feel your hand from the far side of the bed. Pushing my head forward. The cock nearing, then inside my mouth.

'Suck him. I want him hard again.'

I close my eyes and comply.

'Ask for it.'

'Please, ma'am, may I suck his dick?'

'Of course, bitch.'

Your hand grips my hair, holding me in place. My hands flat on the bed, body twisted at the waist, I am bent forward and it is awkward but I make my way towards him.

The cock fills my mouth. Use my tongue to feel it. Swallowing a mouthful of jizz while I start to suck him. A flash of pleasure knowing that I am sharing him with you. Eating him as you have done before. Enjoying a man when I detest men. All for you and your pleasure, ma'am.

Lips stretch, move along his length. Slightly sticky with your juice and the sperm that was in my mouth. Soon I will have him clean. Work at it diligently, helped by your hand as it pulls my face around, back and forth.

Feel him hardening. Let his cock out of my mouth. Lick along the entire shaft. There is more gooey sticky wetness at his balls, in the crack of his ass.

He has other ideas, or are they yours? He takes hold of his cock and uses it to smear the baby batter on my face, painting me with it. Feel your weight on the bed behind me, then your second hand on my chin. Open my jaw: the cock passes into my mouth as he spreads his semen.

You: pressing against my back now. Feel your breath as your face is close for a good look. Soft breast against my side. Hard nipple offering encouragement in its centre.

My tongue: sticking it out and licking at the cock each time it comes near. Tasting the goo that clings to the shaft, the rest starting to dry. The combined tackiness pulling at my flesh each time he drags it across my cheeks and chin.

Back to complete hardness. Look up at him. Still unable to make his features out but trying in the darkness of the room. Your hands holding my head. He pushes the cock back into my mouth. *Face fuck me.* Suck. Each push a little deeper. He wants to bury it all in me.

'That's my bitch, show him what a good cock-sucker you are. Look how hard you got him so quickly.'

Your words hot in my ear. Making me crazy with lust and sin. I suck him harder. Opening my throat as best I can in this position.

A pop: *in medias res,* he pulls back and out. His wet length flush along my face, shifting; his hairy sac at my mouth. My tongue darts out, measuring, weighing. Rewarded with another taste of *you* along with his musk and sweat.

You: rising up and dropping down. Sandwiched

between the two of you. Locked, as you and he kiss. The cock throbbing on my face.

Time. Unable to move. Limited to giving his balls little kisses and licks.

Yank: hair clenched in your hand, I fall back. Your bodies move forward.

'He better be clean!'

Words sizzling my ear.

You lean over me, taking the cock into your mouth. Watch, excited, seeing his full length disappearing in your mouth. You can do what I cannot: deep throat. You know men better than I do, always have. He grunts. You deep throat him again and again. Heavy breasts swinging above me. Reach up to caress them.

Fingers at my pussy; exploring; pushing. A moan as one works my hot wet depths. My hips moving, needing and wanting. Added pressure as a second hand joins the first. Thicker fingers, one forcefully entering alongside yours. Feet flat on the bed, lifting my hips. Fingers sliding in and out. Sometimes together, sometimes taking turns. Both soaked with my juice which is flowing heavily, running out and down to my ass. Then a finger is in my ass. Is it yours? I hope it is. Two fingers in my ass: both of you. *Fingers everywhere.* A universe of fingers that finger-rape. I am finger-fucked happy.

Bodies moving again. Hair still wrapped in your hand. Pulled to meet your wishes. Both of us on the bed and next to each other. Face at your hip. Watch again as he moves between your legs.

Your free hand guides him into you.

I smell and watch your sex. Him: driving deep and fast, excitement on his face. You lift your legs up so I can see better. *Transfixed by the sight.* The cock exiting wet and slick and oh so hard.

Watch. I watch. You want me to see; you want me to know.

Your hand: jerks my head to the bed. He pulls out and turns. Him: extended over your leg. Wavering in the air. Red, wet, shiny. I start to move; your hand pulls me. Taking it in my mouth again. Sucking it. Tasting your fresh juice again; he fucks my mouth again.

Three minutes, more. Clean it, he moves it back to you. Fucking you faster and harder, pulling back out and allowing me to repeat my cleaning job. Repeat this several times. His need to reach orgasm muted.

He: fucking you for your pleasure now. Nearing it, your hand releases me and I'm free to move and help in other ways.

He's pulled your legs up to your chest, holding them under his arms. He pounds you. Your face clear. Move up and kiss you. Thanking you. Our kiss long and deep. Holding and caressing your face as I kiss you.

'Show him what a good bitch you are.'

'Yes, ma'am.'

Move down again, behind both of you. Sliding under, my tongue meets the cock. It exits your pussy. Licking at it, the balls. Then where it joins with you. Sucking, licking. My finger finds your asshole. Slick with your wetness and moves easily over it.

Directly behind him now. Both hands spreading his ass, trying not to impede his movements. Tongue finds his ass and I lick. *Showing him just how good of a bitch I am for you.* Probing him.

'She's – her – tongue – my ass – *wow.*'

Hear you gasp and know that has pushed you over. Your final moments together, hard and violent.

He: falls back, rolls to the side.

You: panting before me.

'Now clean me, bitch.'

I did not need the order. It was my intention to suck you clean.

Kiss my way up your right leg. Little butterfly kisses with a quick touch of the tip of my tongue every few inches or so. Your body hot, damp with sweat, salty. Tongue tingling. I reach your sex.

Your lips pulled out, long and distended. Your odour intoxicating, strong. Wetness covers your pussy and the lower region of your bush. The sperm leaking out of you.

You raise your hips, allowing me easy access. Lick again and again. Keeping my tongue flat to clean your folds. Each journey ending in the soft, curly fur. Your clit, hard and long, peeks at me. My movement ensures that my tongue travels over it each time. Knowing that it is not what you like best but wanting to delay that for now.

Feeling your digits weave along my scalp, a gentle pressure that guides my mouth back to your wet centre. I slide my tongue into you now. Continue to suck you clean. Forcing my tongue to its extremity inside you, wanting all that you have but finding less and less salty goo. Thinking that it is almost time.

'You can do it now.'

Pull my face back and up. Smiling. Your eyes flash: you see the shine covering my face. I keep my focus on your eyes, open mouth finding your clit at the same time.

Lips surround it. With an increasing suction, I suck on it. So long and hard. Engorged with blood and lust. I make a sound of contentment as I settle my mouth on it. Moving my head up and down, the way you like it. Sucked on like a cock. My lips gripping it, tongue caressing it.

You never fail to drive my wantonness to a higher level and I start to vocalize as I pleasure your pleasureland. Loud humming sounds, knowing the vibrations will send you little shivers as they pass from my lips to your clit. Sucking loud, wet. My mouth releasing so I can talk dirty:

'*Please feed me your big girl-cock.*'

'It's so hard and throbbing in my mouth.'

'Please fuck my face with it. You know how I love when you do that.'

Rub my face from side to side over your wetness. Feeling the raised finger of your womanhood on my cheeks.

'Does he know how you fuck me with this?'

'Stabbing at my clit with it.'

'How I scream out your name when I come.'

Hair is almost ripped out in clumps. You position my mouth where you want it. Your hips pumping up and down. A command: *'Suck me now!'* Fucking my mouth with your clit. Thrusting up, over and over. Hips raising me up, hands pulling me down. Face-fucking your bitch, using her mouth for your sins. My mind swimming in the knowledge that I am your bitch, I receive your sinful desire.

Then *in medias res*: on my back, you above me. Your head thrown back, breasts swinging. You grind down on my face. Rolling your hips. Just as I think you might smother me, I'm flooded with wetness. Washing over and into my mouth. Your body shaking on me. Strong shakes, one after another. Each subsequent wave tapers off until you come to a stop. Your weight leaves me and returns by the length of my body. Covering mine with yours. Our bodies. Nuzzle my nose into your hair. Listening to your breathing slowing, calming, returning to normal. Kiss your head. Hold tight. Our bodies.

My heart: it is pounding but nowhere near the pace of yours; yours is running. Our bodies relaxing, merging. Fitting together. Complete. One. Us. We. You, me.

You: asleep in my arms. Kiss you tenderly, join you in rest.

Your body: it shifts and I roll, following your movement, trying to remain in your warmth. Not awake, half-conscious, eyelids crack open, see you looking into my face. Eyes close again, a smile.

You push me onto my back. I lie among the pillows and covers. Still not ready to leave the comfort of your body, one arm slides under your side just as you start to move over me.

* * *

It is bright in the room. What happened to time?

You hover over me and say: 'Good morning, sunshine.'

I want more sleep. But it doesn't matter what I want.

Your hand cuts across my face. Slapping hard. The force turns my head sideways.

Awake now. Look back up towards you but, before I can speak or see your face, your hand returns. Swift, ambushing; turning my face back into the pillow; fingers stinging along the flesh of my left cheek where your hand has struck.

The weight of your body, heavy, and you reach for

one arm, then the other. Shoving them down along my sides where you trap them with your thighs and knees. Immobile now. See: the firmness in your face. Your gaze: down at me. You hold me like this, your face without emotion for the longest minute in the brightest morning of the earth.

Deliberate slowness: your left arm moves back. Me: fascinated by the way your body moves. The muscles of your upper arm flex, your left breast lifts, your palm, open and flat.

'Bitch!'

A handful of hair yanked and pulled and twisted: you spit the word out.

Hair anchored in your fist, you pin my head. Your body leaning over and tilted to the side. The other arm rising and falling: you continue to slap my face. Sharp claps of pain along with increasing heat as I feel my face reddening from the blows.

Both of your hands ripping at my hair, bouncing my head up and down on the bed.

'*What the fuck did you think you're doing coming here unannounced!*'

'*Sucking my soon-to-be-husband's cock ... and his ass ...*'

'*Where the hell have you been?*'

'*... missed you so much ... hurt ... hurts ...*'

'*You bitch, why are you back?*'

Your hands: they toss my head free and you reach down and twist both my nipples. Nipples that are rock-hard. A fact that did not escape you. You continue to twist and pull them, a wicked grin now on your face.

'Are you wet?'

'Yes, ma'am.'

My pussy: soaked.

A hand flies across my face again.

'Will this make you squirt?'

Eyes wide, focused on your hand clenched into a fist. Thinking that you will hit me, really hit me, with closed fist.

You say no. Open your hand and angle your torso down closer to me. Your face: inches from mine.

'But I will whip you; beat you some more. Make it crystal clear that you are my bitch! Now and for ever; no matter what. And you will never, *ever* leave again.'

Your hips: rotating, undulating back and forth. Feel the heat and wetness of you. You: positioned pussy to pussy with me.

Hands beside my head, rubbing me. Offering my pussy to you and you take it, using it to pleasure your land of pleasure.

'I need to fuck you again. Beating my bitch always gets me hot.'

The pillow behind my head: you tear it away, force it under my ass. Keeping my pelvis up for you.

My mound slick with you as you rub yourself harder and faster on my body. Grind along with you. Pushing upwards and moving in the opposite direction.

A fire in your eyes: *in medias res*, you watch me under you.

'Come on, bitch, you can fuck better than that! Remind me why I like fucking you, why I should continue to fuck you. Why I should keep you after I marry a cock. Give me that pussy ...'

I bring my pussy up. Thrusting it out so that you can work your clit against mine. The friction of your pubic hair against my shaved nakedness. You thrust forward. Long minutes of controlled violence. Your grip on my breasts; it hurts and hurts good. You: relentless, pain-giver. Want to wrap my legs around you, scissor with you. The twinkle in your eyes tells me you are aware of my wanton need. You: taking much pleasure knowing my wants are denied.

'This fuck is all about me.'

'I am the bride.'

'I make the decisions around here.'

You are the decider, ma'am.

I know that I am yelling but I don't know what or how loud. You fall forward: hooking your arms around my shoulders. Your teeth closing in the soft flesh of my shoulder.

* * *

105

I am your maid of honour. *Your* wedding. Watch you become one with Don. 'Mrs. Elliott.' How odd. Lauren Elliott now. Lauren Silver is gone. I remember our night together, and the nights that will come, as you say the words of fidelity. The cock. Your pussy. The honeymoon. The juices. The smells. One of the bridesmaids smiles at me and I see it in her eyes: they are my eyes, the eyes I once had, eyes I may still have, hope that I have. I know this girl is yours as I am yours.

Don sees this.

We all belong to you; we're all marrying you today.

The Houseboy
Aishling Morgan

'That's the place. She turns up every last Friday of the month at six, regular as clockwork.'

Darren gave a thoughtful nod. If what Al was saying was true, then the story had to be worth five figures. What he needed were details, and pictures.

'And what about the men?' he asked.

'They're ordinary types, businessmen mainly. Nice cars, most of them, so blokes with a bit of money. I got a tip on one numberplate, a custom job. It was bought last year by a guy named Charles Moore. He's a regular, and I've seen him bring mates, three of 'em one time. I reckon she gets off on getting fucked by loads of guys at the same time, or maybe she likes to pretend she's a whore? Or maybe she's into that Jap business, *bukkake*, you know, when the girl kneels down to give a load of men blow jobs and they all spunk in her face.'

Al finished with a dirty grin and Darren found himself imagining the beautiful Isobel de Vraine on her knees in a circle of men, her face plastered in spunk. It was the exact opposite of her public image as the perfect ice-cold beauty, the woman who everybody wanted and nobody could have. In the two short years since she'd shot to fame she'd turned down one well-heeled and handsome male celebrity after another, leading to speculation that she was a lesbian. Research into her background had drawn a blank, except for one intriguing fact. Once a month she would visit a lonely house, a house that was also visited by a suspiciously large number of single men. Something had to be going on, and whoever got the story was going to pocket a lot of money. Al had done his research well, keeping ahead of the competition, but it was only a matter of time before the facts came out, either through another reporter or when one of the men got greedy and decided to go direct to the papers.

The house was immediately across the valley from the lane where they'd parked their cars. It stood completely alone, nearly half a mile from the nearest neighbour and surrounded by tall trees. Only the upper two storeys were visible, with two lines of windows showing beneath a hotch-potch of gables and little, red-tiled roofs. It looked a bit ill-kempt, but whoever owned it had to have money, or be doing something to earn it, and the address didn't show up anywhere in the business listings or on the net.

All they'd been able to discover was that it belonged to a Mrs Anne Taylor. Darren turned to Al.

'What about the woman, this Mrs Taylor?'

Al shrugged. 'Search me. Some old friend, I suppose. She's discreet, or she'd have come to us already. That's why I haven't approached her. All I know is what I've seen. She's built like a brick shit-house and she dresses like it's the 50s.'

'How old is she?'

'Thirty-five, forty tops.'

Darren went quiet once more. He didn't know as much as he'd have liked to, but if there was one thing he'd learnt in his ten years digging out the seedy secrets of the rich and famous it was that you had to move fast. He'd meant to stay with Al just long enough to confirm that it really was Isobel de Vraine who arrived, and maybe sneak a few pictures, but with what they'd found out it might just be possible to get more, perhaps everything they needed.

'I'm going to try and get inside,' he announced. 'I'll tell her I'm a mate of this Charles Moore. That should do it.'

'What are you going to use for a cam?' Al asked.

Darren grinned and tapped at his watch, a bulky gold and steel affair that concealed a minute but high-quality lens and the works of a digital camera. Al grinned.

'Nice one. Go for it. Call me when you're out and I'll meet you at the Ring o' Bells.'

Darren didn't waste time. A five-minute drive brought him to where a narrow, unpaved lane led down to the old house. Only one other vehicle stood outside, an ancient but well kept Morris Oxford, the black paintwork gleaming with polish and the chrome showing no more than a few small blemishes. He parked his own car next to it and climbed out, trying to push himself into role as a nervous new punter as he looked around.

It was no surprise Al had had difficulty finding out what was going on. The house was completely surrounded by a thicket of rhododendrons with mature limes and beeches rising among them, shielding it from the view of all but the most determined. At the back the ground rose steeply, so much so that only the rooftops were visible from the road, while beyond the trees a ploughed field stretched down to the valley bottom. The house itself seemed to loom above him, and it was all too easy to imagine eyes looking down at him from the upper windows, while the worn yellow stone façade and the massive, black-painted front door added to the sinister air of the place. Darren had to brace himself before stepping forward, and he had no difficulty in appearing nervous as he rang the old china doorbell.

He expected a long wait, and jumped back when the door swung open almost immediately to reveal a woman of imposing physique. She was not far short of six feet tall, with broad shoulders and a truly massive

bosom, while her waist would have seemed thick had it not flared to extraordinarily broad hips. A suit of tan-coloured tweed worn over an old-fashioned blouse and set off with a double string of pearls gave her a look as respectable as it was outdated. It was the last thing he would have expected for a woman who apparently ran a brothel, but he couldn't help but note that the stockings encasing her big but impressively long legs were seamed at the back, while her highly polished, knee-length boots of fine brown leather sported three-inch heels. As he was on the steps leading up to the door she was looking down on him from such a height he immediately felt small and somewhat intimidated, a sensation her voice did nothing to dispel.

'Are you the houseboy?' she demanded.

'Yes,' Darren answered automatically. 'You must be Mrs Taylor. Charles said ...'

She didn't bother to let him finish but turned on her heel, allowing Darren to follow her into a high-ceilinged hallway, decorated in a style he hadn't seen since he visited his grandparents' house as a child. To one side a broad staircase led up to a landing half-shrouded in gloom. Mrs Taylor started up and Darren followed, not at all sure what was going on but thrilled to have got inside so easily. She spoke again as they reached the landing, where a second staircase to the upper storeys led up to a closed door.

'Go up to the top floor. You'll find your clothes laid out in the dormitory. Be sure to dress properly, as I'll want to inspect you when you've completed your first task, which is to clean the servants' bathroom.'

Darren nodded in response. She clearly thought he knew what was going on, which made it essential that he didn't give himself away by saying the wrong thing, even though her remarks were extremely puzzling. He followed her up the second flight of stairs, at the top of which she opened the door onto what seemed to be a granny flat but might well have had some less respectable purpose. The carpet within was red, and on the opposite wall was a picture of a voluptuous woman wearing nothing but thigh boots and carrying a whip.

'You have one hour precisely,' Mrs Taylor told him and closed the door behind her.

A heavy click signalled that she had locked him in, leaving Darren feeling as nervous as he was triumphant as he began to explore. It was blatantly obvious that the upper part of the house was designed for sex parties, and that could only mean his suspicions were correct and that Isobel de Vraine was engaged in something the public were going to be very keen on indeed. It didn't look as if it was just ordinary sex either, because the pictures on the walls suggested something distinctly kinky, and unusual in other ways. All of them were erotic prints, and all of them showed well-built, sexually aggressive women, some alone, some in company with smaller, meek-looking men. None of them were modern, and none of them showed any sex acts as such, although in one or two the men had their hands tied behind their backs or were being beaten across their buttocks.

Darren began to take photographs, with his imagination running ever hotter for the possibilities the place presented. All of the rooms contained beds, big, square four-posters or luxurious divans, upholstered and madeup in crimson and black, but most also contained more intriguing articles of furniture – a cage; a massive cross fitted with leather straps; several stools apparently designed to leave a victim in a comfortable position for whipping and a number of alarming-looking devices of less obvious function. He photographed everything, and with each new discovery his imagined earnings rose, until by the time he had found the room hung with whips, canes, rope and chain on every wall he was thinking not five figures, but six. All he needed was one picture of Isobel de Vraine in such surroundings and he was made.

Half an hour had passed before he climbed to the top storey, expecting more of the same, or worse if that was possible. He was disappointed at first as, while the earlier rooms had been luxurious, these were austere to say the least. The floor was bare boards, scrubbed smooth and apparently bleached, while what little furniture he could see was old and cheap. Only when he reached what was obviously the dormitory did his interest quicken once more, as between the two rows of iron-framed beds stood another of the whipping stools, set out at the exact centre of the room with a crook-handled school cane hanging from a hook on one side.

'She's not using that on me,' he muttered to himself, 'and what the fuck are these?'

On the bed closest to the window was a set of clothes: a pair of baby-pink high heels, stockings in the same shade, a pair of ludicrously frilly panties to match, a white pinny and a bobbed blond wig. As he remembered what Mrs Taylor had said he realised that she was expecting him to dress up in the awful things, and that if he didn't, his cover would be blown. He hesitated, imagining himself as he'd look, not merely ridiculous but utterly emasculated. And yet if he could somehow get a photograph of Isobel de Vraine alongside him, or preferably another man, with her dressed like one of the women in the pictures on the floor below he'd be able to name his own price.

Still he hesitated, but the thought of the money won out. He began to strip, hurriedly, while telling himself that at least nobody else who mattered was going to see. That only went so far to quell his feelings of humiliation as he pulled on the frilly panties and the stockings, tied the pinny in place around his waist and pushed his feet into the girly high heels. Mrs Taylor was going to see, and would doubtless enjoy the sight, and as he put on the wig he was promising himself that he would make her life a misery once he had the photographs he needed.

A large, plain mirror stood on one wall and he found himself unable to resist looking at his reflection, or making a few small adjustments to his outfit before realising the implications of what he was doing and telling himself forcefully that he didn't care if his thigh-high, pink stockings were straight or not. Instead he told himself that there was at least one good thing about the outfit, because the wig made him look so different, and so feminine, that even if he was forced to take pictures of himself with Isobel de Vraine and unedited copies somehow got out, he would not be easy to recognise.

Thinking of his intended target, he checked his watch, to find that while there was nearly an hour until she was due to arrive Mrs Taylor would be coming upstairs in just a few minutes. She'd said something about cleaning the servants' bathroom, which he quickly identified as a small room containing a huge, cast-iron bath, a sink and a single chair of the same bleached and scrubbed wood as the floor. There was a scrubbing brush, a bucket and a large green bar of carbolic soap on the window sill, while the floor was marked with dirty footprints and the bath had a dull brown tidemark, as if somebody had used it after coming in from a game of rugby or a cross-country run.

Darren hesitated, none too happy about having to even

pretend to do menial tasks, but it was evidently what Mrs Taylor would be expecting of him. With a heavy sigh for the difficulties of his working day he turned on the hot tap and began to fill the bucket. The bath was going to be easy, the floor less so, while he could imagine just how he'd look bending over in the frilly pink knickers, never mind crawling on his hands and knees as he did the floor. He stopped work, telling himself it would be all right as long as he looked busy when the awful woman came upstairs.

He didn't have long to wait. Her heavy tread sounded on the staircase just moments later, and as he heard the boards of the landing creak he began to scrub at the tidemark in the bath. She appeared in the doorway, dressed as before, her face stern, then sterner still as she took in the scene.

'What is this?' she demanded. 'You've barely begun. I expected you to be finished by now, young man.'

Darren found himself making excuses by reflex.

'I'm sorry, Mrs Taylor, but ...'

'No excuses!' she boomed, her voice so loud and so full of menace it made him wilt inside. 'When I tell you to do something I expect it done, and done properly. Well, there's only one way to treat a lazy houseboy, isn't there?'

'Er ...,' Darren began, thinking of the whipping stool and the cane in the dormitory and desperately seeking a way out that wouldn't give him away. 'I'm sorry, Mrs Taylor, I really am. I'll do it properly, I promise.'

'Yes,' she interrupted, 'you will do it properly, once you've been given a sore bottom to teach you what happens to lazy, slovenly houseboys. Over my knee with you!'

She'd been advancing on him as she spoke, until they were both standing beside the chair. Darren had been expecting her to tell him he was going to get six-of-the-best with the cane, and was taken completely by surprise as she sat down and hauled him after her. He went across her knees, able to manage only a brief cry of protest and then another of pain as his arm was twisted hard into the small of his back.

'Yes,' she went on, 'over my knee for a good, old-fashioned spanking, that's what happens to naughty houseboys, isn't it? And that's what you're going to get!'

'No, look, I ...,' Daren wailed, only to break off as one massive hand came down across his buttocks. 'Ow! Mrs Taylor, please!'

He tried to struggle, but she was extraordinarily strong. While he squirmed in her grip and her hand descended across his bottom for the second time, he desperately tried to tell himself that he needed to play his part in order to get what he wanted. That didn't make the punishment any easier to take: the awful knowledge burning in his head that he was being spanked across a woman's knee was no less painful than the repeated smacks of her hand on his bottom.

117

'We'd better have these down too, don't you think?' she said, and the situation suddenly became far worse as his frilly knickers were hauled down to bare his buttocks.

The spanking began once more, harder than before and much more painful, while she had tightened her grip on his wrist so that it was all he could do to pretend he was letting her do it for the sake of his scoop rather than because she was stronger and he had no choice in the matter anyway. Smack after smack was applied to his bottom, twenty, then thirty, at which point a horribly embarrassing fact began to filter through his pain. His cock was getting hard.

That was bad enough, as he had never, ever imagined himself as the sort of man who could get turned on by anything so perverted, never mind when he was on the receiving end, but his rapidly growing erection was pressing into Mrs Taylor's leg and she could scarcely fail to notice. Sure enough, after another dozen or so hard spanks she stopped and reached down between his legs, speaking as she grasped the trunk of his cock.

'Why you dirty, filthy little boy! You're getting excited, aren't you? Why you disgusting little pervert! This is supposed to be a punishment and your dirty little willy's getting hard! Well, I'll just have to spank harder, won't I!'

Her disapproval sounded genuine, but that hadn't stopped her tugging at his now rock-hard cock, or spanking him. She merely let go of his wrist and began to use her left hand to apply the smacks, while masturbating him with her right. That meant he was no longer being held down, but Darren was too far gone to resist. It had been altogether too long since any woman had touched him at all, and there was no denying how good it felt to have his cock pulled, or the effect the spanking was having on him. Despite the raging shame in his head he stayed down, trying desperately to concentrate on being masturbated by a woman and not to think of the fact that he was over her knee for a spanking or that he was dressed up in pink, girly underwear and a pinny. Unfortunately she had other ideas.

'I suppose you like to dress up as a girl?' she demanded, now spanking with all her strength and tugging furiously on his straining cock. 'I suppose you do it all the time, parading about in women's underwear. Well, my boy, it's not supposed to be exciting, it's supposed to be to humble you, to make you understand your place while you go about your chores, just like having your bottom smacked is supposed to punish you. But oh no, you like it, don't you, you filthy little sissy, you ...'

She broke off with an exclamation of disgust as Darren finally gave in to his feelings and spunked up down her legs and all over the floor. That didn't stop the spanking though, or the motion of her hand on his now slippery cock, but she continued until he'd been milked dry and hung limp and panting across her knees. Only then did she speak again, her voice suddenly gentle and soothing.

'I suppose we might have known that would happen. It always does when dirty little boys like you get carried away, and I have to admit that you've got me all hot and bothered. Now I trust you're going to say thank you without any fuss?'

Darren didn't answer, too full of shame and of relief to find words for his emotions, while he had no idea what she meant anyway. Even as she eased him down to the floor he was thinking it was all over, only for her to take a firm grip on his hair as she started to tug up her skirt. At that he tried to speak, but only managed a weird gulping noise as he was pulled forward, kneeling in his own spunk, his head directed down into the V of her open thighs.

She had no knickers on. Her plump, hairy cunt showed naked between her thighs, the slit wet with excitement, her clitoris a glossy bulge already poking out from beneath the heavy hood. He tried to fight, not her, but his own feelings, but for the second time in quick succession he failed utterly and allowed his face to be pulled in close to the musky flesh of her sex and immediately began to lick. His cock was still dribbling spunk, but he couldn't stop himself from putting his hand to it, tugging at the limp yet sensitive flesh as he licked the woman who'd spanked him.

The real reason he was there had been pushed to the back of his mind as she began to moan and pulled his head in between her thighs more firmly still. There he was, on his knees in a puddle of his own spunk, in heels and cheap, pink nylons, his frilly pink panties pulled down behind to expose his smacked bottom and his limp cock jiggling in his hand as he made a pathetic attempt to masturbate. She came, full in his face, as he was still pulling at his now half-stiff cock and letting out a feeble dribble of spunk. She ground her cunt into his face for her own powerful orgasm.

Darren was left weak and panting, but slowly the true purpose of his visit came back to him. Isobel de Vraine would be arriving shortly, presumably to join in with another round of punishment and humiliation for him. The thought of her doing anything at all to him was enough to make him wish he hadn't come, but that wasn't the only reason he went to work with a will when Mrs Taylor order him to clean up the mess on the bathroom floor. She'd done something to him, bringing him to a level of ecstasy he'd never experienced before and which he was determined to find again.

As he scrubbed at the floor, he was already planning visits to several of the beautiful dominatrices he'd come into contact with over the years, not those he'd exposed, but the ones he'd paid to betray clients. He was even wondering if he'd be able to negotiate discounts when at last the bell rang. Mrs Taylor had been watching him clean up and spoke in sudden alarm, her voice very different to the commanding tones she'd used before.

'Oh dear, that must be my niece, Isobel. She doesn't know anything about this at all, so you'd better run along. Don't worry, you're quite safe up here, so you can tidy yourself up, but you'd better nip out the back so she doesn't see you. Oh, and one other thing, as you're new, and I hate to bring up what might be an unpleasant subject, but in my line of work a girl has to take precautions. Our little session has all been recorded.'

Teasing Timmy
Primula Bond

Christ, we're bored.

It's not supposed to rain in Devon. There's a limit to how much decorating you can do to spruce up your idyllic country cottage for renting, before you're yearning for the doorbell or the phone to ring. But the job has to be done, and fast, otherwise our investment will have been wasted. In the absence of glittering visitors from London to entertain us, and also any sensible overalls, Jane and I have taken to dressing each day in ludicrous, inappropriate fairytale clothes, just to make each other laugh.

Today I'm Mother Hubbard, wearing nothing but a flowery pinny. Jane is Goldilocks in a see-through baby-doll. We've tarted up nearly every room except the sitting room, which is full of paint pots, brushes and fabric swatches.

Just as we're finishing our doorstep ham sandwiches

and apple crumble, there's a rapping on the front door. We both drop our spoons in surprise. Jane is up first, smoothing the silk negligee down and flicking her yellow hair. A flush of excitement mounts her cheeks. I follow close behind her. Perhaps at long last those rough, tough locals have sniffed us out. It's been bloody weeks since either of us had a man.

'Oh no, you don't,' I growl, pushing past my mate. 'It's my turn. You shocked the postman quite enough yesterday.'

I dash through the sitting room, the pinafore flapping between my legs. My back is cold.

'Sally Seaman? You called us last week. About the property feature? We're from *Cute Cottages*. But we seem to have come at a very bad time.'

A tense-looking peroxide blonde in a tight, pink suit is on the doorstep, accompanied by a spindly young man in a striped jumper and clutching a camera. They are both staring openly. Well, I am practically naked, and Jane is totally see-through. We're both shivering as the wind nips past our visitors to get inside the warm house.

'Sal?' Jane glares at me. 'What's this about a feature?'

'Yeah, I forgot to tell you.' I shrug. 'But think about it. It'll be brilliant publicity once it's in the rentals section.'

'And it's good to have company. At last.' A slow smile stretches across Jane's face. 'We've been starved, haven't we?'

I nod, grinning. We turn back to face our visitors.

'Come in, come in,' we chorus, throwing the door open wide. 'Now is a very good time indeed!'

We prod the prim, unsuspecting magazine writer off the doorstep, and nudge the callow photographer, leading him into the cottage.

'There's so much to show you,' says Jane, lifting her arms so the baby-doll rides right over her tanned thighs. Little minx is wearing no knickers. 'We think we've made it contemporary, yet enticing. We want people flocking here to unwind, you know? Relax.'

The boy is bright red, pushing his dark hair nervously off his face with long fingers and staring straight at Jane's big, red nipples poking through the flimsy material. She looks gorgeous. A wet dream on a wet day. I can see a bulge stretching his smart trousers. My stomach tightens

'This is the main sitting room, which of course we will be stripping to its bare essentials,' Jane chatters, gesticulating about the room. She pushes the two of them onto the sofa, right on top of the little damp patch where I was lying this morning, watching telly and masturbating with one of the paintbrushes, using the soft bristles to fire me up, stroking them across my tender sex, tickling my clit, then using the long, blunt handle to push up me, take the place of a real, live, throbbing cock. Oh, yes. Not even my sweet Jane knows about that ... yet.

But for now I'm standing meekly beside her while she twitters and twirls and absently reties the apron strings so that a big bow now covers my bottom.

'Coffee?' I suggest, turning to walk into the kitchen and displaying my naked backside.

'As you can see, Sal's very domesticated,' laughs Jane, stroking my bottom as I pass her. 'We're a good pair, actually. I'm the creative designer; she's the dogsbody.'

'I heard that!' I cough in protest, returning with two mugs of coffee. Jane drapes her arm across the mantelpiece, cocking her leg so that we can all see the red slice of her bare cunt.

'Think I look like an art deco figurine?' she asks, tilting her chin in profile.

'More like a naff shepherdess you could buy in Poundland,' I mock, reaching to tug her negligee down over her legs and deliberately brushing against her waxed snatch. She flinches and squeals, batting at my hand. I know it's with pleasure, not embarrassment, but our guests won't know that. The tip of her tongue pokes between her teeth. I come closer, put my hand on her hair, make as if to kiss her, then she twists her head towards our audience as if we're forgetting.

'Great coffee,' croaks the photographer. The lady features writer slowly crosses one plump thigh over the other with a swish of stocking and flips her notebook to a blank page. The photographer hasn't even taken off his

126

lens cap. He's huddled next to her on the sofa, clutching his mug between his bony knees and rocking slightly.

'Light the fire, would you Sal?' Jane asks, smiling over my head at the visitors.

'Of course, darling.' I bend over the hearth like a parlour maid, fiddling with the kindling and displaying the shadow of my slightly parted bottom like it's some kind of jungle mating ritual.

'Lovely real fire, even in summer,' remarks Jane, stroking her toe lazily up my leg. 'It makes you want to just lie down on this rug, get some big hunky bloke to fuck you right here in front of the flames, you know? Especially when the weather is so shitty. We never close the curtains. No need for that kind of privacy out here in the country. Open house, you see, for all gentleman callers.'

I laugh quietly, get down on my knees now. 'We live in hope.'

The lady clears her throat.

'So if you love the cottage so much, why do you want to change it?'

'Well, it needs updating. All very well being characterful, but it still needs to have all the contemporary touches, especially in the kitchen and bathrooms. That's what tenants expect in their love shacks these days. Somewhere they can come for a really dirty weekend. And the décor when we bought it was, well, more chintz than chutzpah, know what I mean?'

'Sure.' The lady is writing something down, crossing her legs again and definitely wriggling. 'So it's only one bedroom?'

'Yes. Adults only. It'll make a sexy love nest for someone,' I pipe up, lighting the fire then sitting back to smooth my hands over my breasts, down over my hips, leaving sooty stripes all over my pinny. The photographer gulps his hot coffee down too fast.

'Yes. So what we really want to create is a place where really hot people will want to come, you know, rut like goats all weekend in the soft beds, here on the rug, out under the cherry tree, down on the beach, then go back to work satisfied. Or a bunch of girls, hen night maybe, could go looking for the hoary locals. I've heard they're hung like donkeys!'

'Not enticed them over the threshold so far, though, have we?' I brush at the soot marks, making my breasts jump and bounce over the bib front. Absently I rub at my hidden nipples, biting my lip with pleasure at the sharp response. 'I mean, Jane and I love each other like crazy and girl on girl action is hot, especially on a rainy afternoon, but you know, a red-blooded woman needs a good, hard cock occasionally, not just her best mate's tongue and tits.'

'That's exactly it. A good, hard cock,' Jane echoes thoughtfully, swinging her leg about so that her slit visibly opens and closes like a little mouth. She tilts her head as if the idea is occurring to her for the first time. 'That's all we need, to make this place complete.' She allows a pause. 'Not shocking you, are we?'

Our guests shake their heads hard, as if they're trying to empty them, and make various humming and *aahing* noises. The sparky-looking woman seems to have lost the power of speech. But it's not her we're interested in. We both focus on the young photographer. His hair needs a trip to the barber for a decent hair cut and shave, but he's so deliciously young and, when you examine him closely, he has beautiful green eyes, spaced far apart, and jutting cheek bones like Rudolf Nureyev.

'Good. So all we're saying is, we need some fresh meat. Young, and tender,' I muse, running my hands over the swelling tops of my breasts, pushing them together. 'God, that would be good.'

'You're cute, aren't you?' Janie suddenly walks over to the boy, sits on the arm of the sofa, letting the negligee fall away from her pussy. 'What's your name?'

'Timmy,' he croaks, licking his lips.

'Time then, Timmy, to get out your Hasselblad, don't you think?'

Timmy nods and the lady raises her eyes to examine the old beams. I reach under the pinny, flipping it aside to scratch at my fanny and giving a little moan of pleasure as I do so. Jane keeps her face straight. The lady features writer nibbles her biro and uncrosses her legs again, glancing from Jane to Timmy, who's gawping like a rabbit in headlights.

'I'm sure you want to get to work,' Jane says, catching the lady's eye.

'Perhaps a guided tour?' The lady totters to her feet and holds the notebook in front of her like a shield. She attempts to get into the mood. 'Of your love shack?'

'Absolutely Miss, er …'

'Shona Shaw.'

'Brilliant idea, Shona Shaw,' beams Jane. 'Ready, Timmy?'

But Timmy is looking past her, drooling across the room at me. I've flipped the pinafore right over to one side so that my pink slit is fully visible. Unlike Jane I have kept a neat line of hair curling over the crack. Two fingers separate the soft lips, and the pink flesh glistens as my other hand tiptoes up my thigh. Honestly, our guests are so shocked they can barely move, let alone protest.

Jane's expression hardens for a moment. This encounter has become a competition between us. We've been closeted on our own for too long. One of us always has to be the winner. Usually it's Jane. But then she bows her head, gives a mock curtsey. So this is my gig. It's my turn for a little fun.

I run my tongue over my mouth and moan again. My hand pauses as it reaches the first pubic curl, then I lift one finger and beckon to Timmy. He sits up straight as if he's in a deportment lesson.

'You'll see we've completed the bedroom and the bathroom. There's a lovely attic, too. With a telescope. You can see right over the little harbour.'

Jane winks at me and leads the lady out of the room. Honestly, when we're not fighting, we're fondling. I watch the cute twitching of her pert butt, the cute wet promise of what's tucked in there for me later. Then I get up and sashay across to Timmy. I stand in front of him and untie my pinafore, unhook it from over my head, hold it in front of me like a matador in front of a randy bull. His lanky hair is very neatly combed into a side parting, and I ruffle it with my fingernails. He swipes one hand at it in an automatic tidying gesture, his sleeve far too short for his long arm, and quick as a flash I've grabbed his bony wrist and tied the apron strings round it.

'Got to stop you running away!' I breathe, grabbing his other hand, tying them together like manacles above his head. Then I hook the string round the leg of the heavy table behind the sofa. Timmy is now sprawled on the sofa in front of me, hands tied, legs spread.

Out in the hall Jane is chivvying the shell-shocked lady into a pair of oversized wellies and out into the sopping wet garden, chattering all the while.

'More so that you can get a view of the cottage and its surroundings,' she says, pushing Shona Shaw outside to high-step over the overgrown grass and duck under the dripping branches. 'We haven't done any gardening. We prefer the meadow look. Do take your time out here. I'll just nip back inside, see what Sally's up to.'

I see her watching me in the doorway, arms folded. She doesn't trust me. The breeze from the front door shivers over me, naked as I am, hardening my nipples, pricking up my skin.

'Want to taste a horny older woman, Timmy?' Keeping my eyes on my Janie, I kneel up on the sofa, straddling my captive, pushing my pussy into his face.

But Jane isn't missing out on this rare piece of male totty. She walks to the table above his head, leans over it, her juicy tits dangling down. I try to push her out of the way, but I'm distracted by having Timmy lying helpless under me, feel his quick, hot breath on my cunt, the jut of his nose against my clit, and I push harder, burying his face in my sex. As I do so Jane, knowing this will knock the fight out of me, leans down to kiss me.

Timmy starts to lick – what else can he do? His eager tongue slides up my crack, and Jane kisses me, opening her mouth to suck at my lips and my tongue. Timmy knocks me slightly with the urgent force of his lapping, and I lift myself very slightly away from him, push myself back, feel his tongue stretching to get at me.

Jane pulls away. 'Something going begging down here.' She breathes coarsely, pointing at Timmy's trousers. 'A great big porker just ripe for the taking. Which one of us is going to have it, do you think?'

I grin, my lips wet with Jane's saliva. She may be competitive, but she's also fair.

'We'll take turns, of course. We'll both get a good fucking out of this boy's cock.'

Shona Shaw passes the window. A burst of rain has started and her neat hairdo is all messed up. She's pulling the collar of her jacket up, patting at her hair. She stops, right there in the rain, when she sees what we're doing to her assistant.

Jane climbs up on the table and leans right over, so that now I've pulled away her tits are dangling in Timmy's face where my pussy was. She swings them back and forth in front of his mouth. I know what that's like. Those juicy nipples like raspberries, dangling just out of reach, so warm and hard when you get them between your teeth, the reward you get for pleasuring her. He's licking his lips, swallowing frantically, trying to reach the nipples she's offering him.

But it's his cock I'm after now. I can suck her nipples and she can suck mine, any time. This guy is just passing through. I take hold of his trousers and yank them down. Christ, he's huge and totally hard. The young ones are always the best, always ready, always willing, always able, and always able to do it again, and again.

He jerks upwards, perhaps a little anxious, his cock

133

flopping heavily against his stomach. The apron strings are biting into his skinny wrists, so I take pity and cup his balls for a moment, gasping with laughter as he flinches and groans with pleasure.

Jane, panting now, lowers her tits, squashes them into his face, and excitement shoots through me to see his wet mouth closing round one taut nipple and biting hard onto it. I know how she likes that. I know how wet it makes her.

My pussy is twitching frantically, wet from his mouth and wet from excitement, and I can't hold back any longer. Jane isn't so bothered about being fucked, though she enjoys it when it happens. She's the one who taught me all about girls, but I'm the one who goes berserk without a good, hard cock every once in a while. That's why she's letting me have Timmy first. Despite her bossiness, I know she'll do anything for me.

But I want her too. We've been cocooned in this cottage for so long, I'm used to fondling her whenever I like. Timmy's cock is so big that I can ease the swollen tip inside me and still be on a level with Jane's little face as she leans to press her tits into his mouth. I can still kiss her as our prisoner sucks at her, as his cock grows even bigger just for having me spinning on it. My knees are shaking with the effort of keeping myself above him, but kissing Jane is the cream on the cake for me, sucking on her tongue while I make a boy fuck me.

'Now, Timmy,' I murmur, tongue tangled with hers, 'where were we?'

I move very slightly, slipping him further inside. He thrusts eagerly and I pull away teasingly. My toy. Jane squeezes her breasts together, brushes her nipples over his mouth, while I relent and rock gently, up and down, easing slowly down until his cock fills me. I tickle his balls softly again and he groans, muffled by the twin mounds of Jane's breasts.

'What a thing to tell your mates, honey,' I murmur, keeping above him, gripping him with my cunt, holding onto his shoulders, kissing my Jane. 'Pounced on by two hot country bunnies.'

To keep him in place I have to do the work, keep moving and tilting, almost dancing up his length as I start to engulf him. My pussy lips nibble, just as my mouth is nibbling Jane's, and the excitement is overwhelming.

Once or twice his cock nearly slips out again, so I make tiny, fast movements, plunging harder onto him, pulling Jane's head down so I can keep kissing her. He's groaning loudly now. Jane's nearly suffocating him. I'm working him like an instrument, mercilessly using him, and all he can do is lie there, tied to our table, while I luxuriate in the knowledge that I could keep him there all day if I wanted to. Our sex toy.

Doubt he's ever done this before, had two women writhing all over him. I bet he thinks he's died and gone to heaven. Imagine what he'll tell the boys down the pub! He's groaning and swearing, losing what little control he had, bucking furiously under me as Jane starts to moan as well. I wonder if she's fingering herself, but when I glance I see she's released one of his hands from my apron strings and is impaling herself on his free fingers. Christ, that's so dirty, using him like that, it makes me grind even more furiously, his cock right up me now, my hands squeezing her breasts too, pushing them into his mouth, soft and warm, my cunt gripping his cock and clenching.

And watching us through the window there's the white, rain-lashed face of Shona Shaw, her mouth a shocked O.

We all speed up, excitement mounting. Timmy's cock is hard inside me and he's starting to come, I can tell. His cock is swelling and pumping, and I can't help it, I'm grinding down on him, faster, faster, lapping at Jane's mouth, knowing she's being fucked by his fingers. We're all in ecstasy, bands of excitement tighten inside me, and then he comes. I come too, with his spunk spurting up me, making me scream into Jane's face, hearing Timmy's muffled yell as she stuffs her nipples further into his mouth and gives one of her sexy, shuddering climactic moans.

I roll off him. Jane jumps quickly round to lie next to me on the sofa. Timmy looks at us embracing each other. His mouth is drooling open. He stares at his wilting cock.

'Are you all right, Timmy?'I ask him, twining my fingers in Jane's hair.

'Ready to start again?' Jane adds, reaching forwards and wrapping her fingers round his prick. 'Come on, you know you want to. And you haven't done it for me, yet.'

He flushes scarlet, yanks his hand out of the remaining tie, his cock out of her fondling fingers, and scrambles to his feet, muttering to himself and hopping about trying to zip up his trousers.

Shona Shaw is in the doorway. 'Job done, Timmy?'

'Oh, fuck, no,' mutters Timmy, sidling towards her. 'I haven't got the shots yet.'

Shona's yellow hair is in tendrils round her face. Her pink jacket is clinging to her surprisingly big breasts. Her skirt is too tight.

'Give me the camera, Tim.'

He rubs his hair, tugs at his fraying sleeves.

'Sorry, Shona. I'll get to it right away.' He stumbles past me and Jane, still in a disshevelled huddle on the sofa. He picks up the Hasselblad, but Shona steps across and snatches it from him. She slings it round her neck then pushes him back towards me and Jane.

'Yes, you'll get to it all right, but not taking photographs. I want you to remember your manners. One of our hostesses hasn't had the full treatment. Go over there, get those trousers off, and give her one.'

We all three stare at her in amazement. Then, as she

raises the camera, removes the lens cap with a decisive click, and starts to focus it, Jane is the first to move, unzipping Timmy's trousers, pulling out his cock, dipping her head to suck it, pulling away to show us, and the camera, how it's already semi-erect.

'Good, go ahead, get fucking, a threesome, on that lovely big, squashy sofa in front of the fire!' Shona Shaw is dancing with excitement on the carpet as we slowly start to kiss and fondle, push and thrust. 'These pictures are going to make us a fortune!'

* * *

I must have fallen asleep, because I'm roused by a frantic whispering at the door, and a creak of floorboards and the rubbery sound of discarded wellies.

'I should say that's a wrap, wouldn't you, Timmy?' Jane giggles softly, and we're off in uncontrollable laughter. 'Got what you needed, Shona?'

Shona plucks at her assistant's ragged sleeve. 'Absolutely everything, thank you,' she says, flushing. 'Time to get back to town, Timmy. We need to get a hotel.'

Timmy troops obediently after her, throwing a yearning look over his woolly shoulder. I run my finger down my cunt, where he's just been, then lick it like a lollipop.

'I dare you. Give Shona one, Timmy,' I call after him. The door slams behind them, and we rush to the window. Shona is wagging her finger at Timmy as he, aware that we're watching, attempts to accelerate the car manfully over the pot holes in our lane.

Jane climbs on top of me, rubs her sore nipples into my face. 'That's our man quota for today,' she growls, writhing against my pussy. 'I need some girly loving now.'

I laugh, licking one cute nipple. 'Shona'll be so horny after watching all that, I bet she'll have Timmy for dinner, bed *and* breakfast!'

Safe-Word
Ashley Hind

My readers know me as Daisy Tridstone, although
that is only the name I use as a columnist for the *Two
Counties Echo*. I contribute on a daily basis but I am best
known for my weekly piece entitled ''Tis Sad'. In this I
wistfully bemoan the loss of traditional rural ideals to
the onslaught of modern life. It all sounds rather twee,
although I am anything but. It's all anagrams, you see.
The quaint title of my column is actually an anagram
of 'Sadist'. My *nom de plume* is merely the jumbled-up
letters of the phrase 'One Dirty Sadist', an epithet given
to me by a fellow Domme. She had just watched me
whip a girl who, at my command, was fucking herself
with a freshly peeled corn on the cob.

However, my name must now change. The story I give
out will be that I have married. This will no doubt perplex
my bosses, who are both privy to my real name and also

correctly suspect that I am a lesbian. They think me odd anyway, so they may put it down to my usual whimsy. Or perhaps they will blame the menopause, although I'm still a few years off that. Whatever they think, and however potentially damaging a sudden name change is to a writer dependent on a loyal readership, I must still make the alteration. My new name is also an anagram, but not one that I have chosen. From now on I am to be known as Daisy Everrlast.

A Mistress must have a bitch and until very recently I had two. Angel was one – a skinny dyed-blonde with a little, pert arse. She originated from South America. Venezuela, I think. She started as my cleaner and graduated to becoming my only ever live-in slave. There are very few indignities she has not suffered at my hands over the years. As well as being a masochist, she has a profound toe fetish, so as an occasional reward for taking her pain and humiliation I let her worship at my feet. She used to belong to a chubby Domme called Jocelyn, until I took her away. This was cruel, especially as Jocelyn was only young and Angel was her first slave. It was doubly cruel because there may well have been strong feelings developing between Mistress and Slave, certainly more than I was ever prepared to invest. Jocelyn had the size, and was pretty for a big girl, but she was no match for me. Her inexperience told, and she had to bow to my greater influence in the world we revolved in, and to the irresistible power of my delectable tootsies. She had no choice other than to take her loss with mute acceptance.

But hell hath no fury ...

My 'theft' of Angel caused a few ructions within the clubs I frequented. I overreacted to these with vitriolic verbal assaults that eventually saw me ostracised. I didn't care too much. I had no time for petty friendship and grudging respect. I wanted only to be adored and to be so utterly essential to someone that they let me do whatever I chose to do to them, and loved me for it. For my part I would feed, clothe and shelter that person, and let them be my plaything. I couldn't manage any love in return. It was always beyond my selfish needs.

For the most part I derived pleasure from humiliating my girls. The power to make someone do whatever you want is an awesome one, especially if it is absolutely against their will. I got huge satisfaction from making them wallow in degradation. I would delight in forcing poor Angel to endure public indignities, travelling miles to random locations to avoid recognition and repercussions. She used to shake with fear as I drove her around the country, revealing at my leisure the manner in which she would disgrace herself for my benefit. She never got used to it. Each new task made her shrivel with embarrassment. But still the silly girl obeyed, just for the chance to lick my holes or suck her own come off my painted toes.

I can give only a few examples. As time went on they

became ever dirtier, and relating them now they might well come back to haunt me. Once, at a busy public swimming baths, I had her remove her bikini bottoms underwater and shove them up her puss, with half the soaked garment still protruding and visible between her thighs. I then had her get out and walk the long way around the pool perimeter to get back to the changing rooms, where she was forced to flee the enraged staff with only a towel to cover her decency.

On one occasion I took her to a supermarket and had her piss her tight, white ski pants in the bread aisle. She then had to walk up and down each row of the whole store, pretending to be oblivious to the saturation clearly visible to all and spreading down her legs. While doing so she had to choose obviously sexual objects for her basket, such as bananas, courgettes and thick carrots, along with whipped cream and so forth. When she went to pay, she was instructed to loudly announce to the till girl that she had just been fist-fucked by her Mistress, and that her cunt was wetter than it had ever been before.

Another time I drove her to the next town and stopped by the side of a road, where a gaggle of young mums were idly nattering. I stopped and ordered Angel, naked from the waist down except for her shoes, to get out and sit on the hood of the car, less than ten feet from the stunned gathering. She then had to spread her thighs and fuck her pussy with two fingers, as fast and noisily as possible, whilst telling her wide-eyed audience just how much she wanted them all and how desperate she was to lick their lovely arses.

I had planned a similar scenario, only this time she was to get out of the car rubbing her slit, go right up to the mums, and let go a stream of piss all over their legs. I discounted this on the grounds that their outrage would undoubtedly lead to my numberplate being taken, and I didn't want to negate this by parking too far away to witness the whole incident. Similarly, I once aborted my plan to force her to urinate from a theatre balcony onto the opera-watching spectators below, remembering at the last moment that even if she fled without being apprehended, I could still be traced through my credit card box reservation. I did, however, once have her streak onto a nearby golf course and relieve herself into a hole as a group of shocked ladies prepared to putt. These were mild examples of ordeals I put her through. However difficult they were to tolerate, they were still preferable to the beatings I gave her. She could take pain and enjoy it, but I did like to go to town on her defenceless body. In truth her outings of humiliation were often just a way to divert my own bubbling compulsions, a way to sate my desires in less explosive ways, for her sake. I even had to limit my arsenal of weaponry to a few basic canes and paddles so that I could not go overboard. Most times I could contain myself, but every once in a while my passion would erupt in an unrelenting and furious need to hurt her.

Some people see red, but I see purple. Don't ask me to explain because I cannot quite quantify it. I begin to lose control and I am suddenly gripped by a requirement to cause pain in others, and it must be of a sexual nature. All I see in my head is an image of purple, like a soft velvet cloak. It is like I am possessed by the rage of insane Roman emperors. I feel the purple seeping through my body and fizzing in my veins, trying to get out, trying to burst and coat my victim, trying to turn black. All my reason disappears. I snarl and curse and gurgle madly. I am wracked by the urgency to shower my girl in anything I can expel from my body, to cover her. All the while I am doing so, I am infuriated by the fact that my secretions are not the same colour as I see them in my head.

So I beat her and turn her purple that way instead. I slap and cane her beyond anything she can handle. I go on until she is covered in bruises and welts, until her screams evaporate and she drifts into that trance somewhere between bliss and unconsciousness. I vent my fervour until my brain is satisfied that I have enveloped her in my purple shroud. Then, in a final act of release, I savage my own cunt until I come, and collapse beside her, gratified at last. These episodes are thankfully rare. She takes them with her habitual grace, although it can be weeks before she fully recovers.

145

Someone once said my 'turns' were as close as I could get to showing love. They said my need to cover and cloak my girl with what seemed to flow through me was merely a way to convey my protection and desire for that person to be a part of me. Perhaps Angel saw it like this too, but I doubt it. She took the beatings because she was a masochist and because she had to. She had no one else and she knew that as time went on I was becoming more bored of her, tired of that same little arse to take my pleasures from. Angel became more at pains to please me. She had a safe-word but she never used it. I had made it pretty clear that she was of little use to me if she couldn't accept whatever I wanted to give her, so she yielded unquestioningly to my every demand. Nonetheless, familiarity breeds contempt, and eventually I looked for a new girl to supplement my desires.

Cassie made me wet from the moment she nervously approached to ask if there was any chance I could help with getting her work experience at the paper. She was twenty, too plain to be very pretty, but with an attractive innocence that sent twinges to my puss. Her lips were full and soft and her cheeks always a little flushed. She had short, dark hair and large eyes, which often looked shyly at you through her fringe. She was only slightly chubby, but in all the right places. Her breasts were small but so soft, with tiny, pale nipples. She was very conscious of the little roll at her belly but I loved it. Most of all, I loved her behind. It had a pristine newness, lacking the sag and cellulite of Angel's. It was round and soft, big but not fat, and utterly fuckable.

I could tell she was in awe of my authority but I still took my time to seduce her. I let her come to my house to give me examples of her written work. I offered advice and even free tuition. Angel was often present during these visits, although I never formally introduced them. I never troubled to explain the role of the girl who shared my house, thus maintaining the ambiguity of her status. I lived in a small village, and although Angel was known ostensibly to be my domestic help, I had no other visible partner. Rumours regarding my sexuality no doubt flourished. Cassie, living nearby with her parents, must have been aware of any such rumours.

One day I greeted Cassie wearing only my satin gown, having come straight from the shower to receive her. I sat to read her latest efforts, with one knee up on the sofa supporting the papers. My robe was slightly rucked up, giving her an apparently unwitting but actually entirely intentional sneak preview of my neatly trimmed pussy. I could tell afterwards by her flushed features that she had seen it all. When her visit ended by her thanking me and bidding goodbye with a shy peck on the cheek, I knew that she was ready for the taking.

I chose a rather ingenious way to make my final move. Cassie helped her parents run the village newsagents and I sent Angel in one Tuesday morning, knowing that Cassie would be alone. Angel wore a T-shirt and tight leggings only. It must have crushed her to know that she was helping to engineer her own fall from favour. Just before her short walk to the shop, I had her insert her mobile phone right up her quim. I followed and waited outside, peering through the glass unseen to watch Angel enter and pull down her leggings to reveal her bare slit to a dumbstruck Cassie. Then I rang Angel's phone. She let it ring and vibrate inside her six times as previously instructed, and then she slid the glistening phone out and answered it.

'It is my Mistress,' she informed Cassie. 'She wants you.'

I watched Cassie nervously take the juice-wet phone and put it to her ear.

'I have found you a job at the paper,' I said. 'Come to my house tonight to discuss it. Be there at eight sharp.'

She was. By eight-thirty she was lapping at my mushy cunt and by nine my middle finger was deep inside her hot, virgin arse and I was telling her that she now belonged to me. I still tempered my enthusiasm, reining in my lusts for fear of scaring her off before she was completely hooked. Over the first few weeks I treated her almost as a lover, gently introducing her to the world of slavery and of taking spankings to her delicious, plump backside. She liked the tingle and the sting, bucking her newly shaved mons against my thighs, although she would panic as my desire began to take hold and the slaps got heavier, and it was all I could do to pull myself back from the brink.

It is demeaning for a Mistress to admit that she spent hours gorging on the arse of her slave, but I did, although I never let Angel witness it. I was absolutely besotted by Cassie's bottom. It was so warm and tasty, so sweet and tight, the cheeks so yielding as they squashed to my face. I wanted it with worrying eagerness. I wanted to punish it, to hear the slaps burst against it and see it wobble and turn scarlet under my attentions. I wanted it to open before me so I could consume it. I wanted the buns in my mouth and on my face, engulfing me. I wanted to breathe it in, all day and night. More than all of this, I wanted to fuck it.

I eased Cassie into her new life of submission. I paid her attention and granted concessions I would never dream of affording any other girl. I continued to give her the spankings a slave required, but these were only light. She had one brief caning but she used her safe-word almost immediately. I had allowed her this tool of escape to put her at ease, but she called upon it at almost any instant. It left me not only frustrated but also worried that she would prove entirely unsuitable as slave material. The safe-word she chose was *Fanella*. It was the pet-name for her puss, she shyly giggled. With jarring jealousy I learnt

149

it was a name coined by the only other girl she had ever slept with. I was hoping never to hear the word again, but it just kept coming out with alarming regularity. As soon as my fever bit and my mind started running with thoughts of the abuses I longed to bring down upon her gorgeous arse, she would squeak that word and wriggle free as my body sagged with dismay. Later, I would take out my frustrations on Angel, who bore the brunt with her usual acquiescence. In truth, I believe I only kept her around me for these moments. I was tiring of her daily and resenting her more for not being Cassie. I had one girl who I wanted, but gave me nothing, and another I didn't want but would yield everything. Both were pointless. Cassie's bottom taunted me. I needed to take it, to plunder it. I was mocked by its beauty and the hold she had over me. A slave is never yours until she has given up her tightest, most private place. I bought a slimmer dildo for my harness, just to give her an easy introduction. However, each time I slid it from her puss and offered it up to her arse, she would giggle and wriggle and triumphantly proclaim her ridiculous safe-word. Our snatched hours together became increasingly frustrating. I found myself deferring to her pleasure, concentrating on giving her ecstasy in order to encourage her to come to me again. She wanted to play at having me as her Mistress, but she wanted none of the storm that was building inside me to break over her. I knew that once she had enough confidence to strike out on her own then she would leave me. I knew if I didn't make her mine then I would lose her forever.

I planned her subjugation for the next rare occasion she agreed to stay overnight. I gambled with some brinkmanship. I told her straight she was a bad slave. I said if she didn't start obeying me then I would have to let her go, and prayed that she wasn't yet ready to call my bluff. Thankfully, she didn't. She smiled and set about trying to do as I commanded, as I commenced with my detailed scheme for her defeat. I sat her at the dining table and called Angel through with a bowl of steaming chilli con carne. The skinny slave bitch had prepared it under my strict tutelage and it was as fiery hot as I could produce while still keeping it edible. I had particularly ensured that the Dutch chillies were sliced downwards to produce round cross-sections, some still with their hot seeds clinging on. They stood as a bright red visual reminder within the meal of its fiery potency.

Cassie ceased smiling after the first mouthful went in, although she claimed the meal was 'lovely' and did her best to look like she was enjoying it. She knew it was a test and I swelled with joy when I realised that she was trying her hardest to pass it. She pressed on, although she began to sweat and draw in air to try and cool each mouthful. I provided her with beer and gave her licence to drink it at will, knowing full well that it only exacerbated the burn and that milk is the only liquid that can help cut through the heat. She struggled her way through, looking increasingly flustered, until she finally gave up with about a quarter of the portion remaining, her fringe wet with perspiration and her pleas for clemency coming between desperate pants and gasps.

I relented and made her strip so that I could see her sweaty body. I had her sit on the table as I berated her for not finishing the meal, telling her she must be punished for her disobedience. I pressed my fingers into her bare mound and pulled up the skin of her slit to expose the hood of her clitoris and the peeking head beneath. I had Angel pick out one of the remaining hoops of red chilli from the dish, and ordered her to crown Cassie's clit, carefully placing the slice over the delicate flesh to ring the little bud. Cassie breathed hard, waiting for the shock. Then she was yelping and jerking on her perch as the capsaicin burn leached from the pepper and set fire to her clitty, making it swell visibly and stretch the pernicious hoop surrounding it. I held her still, forcing her to tolerate the searing itch.

Her glistening vulva with its pretty adorning red ring looked good enough to spank, so I duly did, three or four times with the flat of my fingers. Although her breath was escaping in tremulous rushes her quim was still not hot enough for my liking, and her dignity was far from demolished. I took the spoon from the puddle of orange-red chilli juice at the bottom of her bowl and pressed the back of it square to the lips of her puss, giving them a light smearing of the spiky sauce. She was now leaning back on her hands, her puss pushed out at me as the heat spread through her delicate parts and little quakes jerked her hips back and forth.

Her gasps and compliance were equally exciting to me and did nothing to temper my rising desire. I wanted to visit my filth upon her. With Angel instructed to hold Cassie's little cunny open, I scooped up a full spoonful of the chilli. I slowly eased it inside my new slave, pushing it in deep before twisting the spoon to deposit the mush inside her. I was still sliding the spoon out as her mouth dropped open and her fluttering breath and jerking hips signalled the spread of the burn within. Her eyes widened and she let out a wail as she saw me reload the spoon, but like a good girl she remained still as I fed her pussy once more. I decided to relent without filling her further and sent her scuttling off to the kitchen with her hand clasped to her crotch, signalling for Angel to assist her. It was easily the most degrading thing Cassie would ever have done, and I watched with sneering glee as she straddled the chrome kitchen bin and held her burning quim open for Angel to delve inside and fish out the remnants of her meal.

'When you are done,' I said, 'you will both come to my room.'

Cassie was flushed and subdued when she came up a few minutes later, and Angel didn't look half as pleased as I thought she would at the humiliation bestowed upon her rival. I had Cassie shower and dry herself off before giving her a quilt and ordering her to sit within my built-in wardrobe. I allowed her to watch me making gentle love to Angel for a while. She was able to silently contemplate the persistent chilli itch inside her while I tenderly kissed my slave helper all over and then slowly fucked her with a smooth strap-on dildo. I reached out and swung the wardrobe door shut on her, so that all she had for comfort were the sounds of my more compliant girlfriend being taken to a series of gentle climaxes over the next couple of hours.

In the morning, still within the confines of the wardrobe, Cassie was served a simple breakfast of tea and toast. This was preceded by a tall glass of hot water and lemon juice, a sure-fire method of cleaning out one's digestive system. I then allowed her to wash and clean her teeth before finally heeding her pleas to let her sit on the toilet. I could already feel the surge of my blood as she sat down, fretting at my refusal to leave her in peace, her crimson face speaking of her urgent need to go. She could hold back no more and had to evacuate in front of me, shivering with the combination of embarrassment and the burn from the chilli for the second time. I made her tell me just how hot it felt. I let her wipe only twice with a moist tissue before my dirty passions took over and I dragged her from her seat, reminding her that it was Angel's job to clean, after all.

The skinny servant who doubled as my fuck-whore was hovering around with the used breakfast plates and turning white with horror at my words.

'That's right,' I said with triumphant malice to the room in general, 'she does as I tell her because if she doesn't then she may as well pack her bags.'

I had Cassie get on all fours on the bed and secured her hands with the leather straps permanently fastened to the headboard. Her moon of a bum was stuck out invitingly and I recall lust gripping me and my control slipping away. With my final vestiges of restraint I gathered my instruments of torture and roughly secured a ball-gag to her thickly salivating mouth. I started with fairly light pinches and smacks to her delicious bottom but the quivering twin jellies of her buttocks just made my juices rush and the purple mist come down. What happened after is all a blur. I know I took my hand to her arse, pussy and legs and only stopped when my palm was stinging. Then I used in turn a whip, a thick belt and a cane. In between blows I pinched and squeezed her flesh, dug my nails into the softness of her thighs, spat on her back and into her shit-crack. I yanked her head back and slapped her face, tugged at her nipples and called her the filthiest names my frenzied mind could think of.

After so many months of moderation towards her my dam just broke. The way her bottom bounced and wobbled as I whipped it or striped it with the cane had me almost screaming with excitement. Her quim was puffy and proud and took my fingers with greater ease than ever, even though she yelled into her ball-gag as I thrust them inside. Taking pain is just a learning process and sometimes you have to be pushed. I could see Angel, ashen-faced and trembling as I made her watch. I goaded her with occasional reminders of her impending task of cleaning the victim with her tongue once I was finished.

The skinny bitch knew well the hurt that Cassie was now experiencing. I could see her flinch as each knew impact landed on my new slave's body. I heard her gasp at the crack of leather on young skin, at the humiliation of my piss torrents splashing over the abused arse, at the saliva-covered back and pulled hair of my delicious girlfriend. Yes, Angel knew exactly how it felt to have my hot urine gushing into her mouth and cascading down her chin. She knew that now my lovely Cassie was being broken in, her own days as my live-in servant were numbered.

My purple passion only grew as I ravished my girl. The sight of her lovely arse just inflamed me and I had to have her, to take her the way I'd dreamt of. She was gabbling into the ball-gag, trying to make her cries coherent. I knew well enough what word she was trying to say but I feigned ignorance.

'What are you saying?' I mocked. 'Are you asking for more?'

I could see Angel beside me getting increasingly agitated at my cruelty, coming close a couple of times to shouting out Cassie's safe-word on her behalf before my menacing glares cut her short. My look carried my threat: speak up now, bitch, and you are finished forever. So with both my girls powerless and at my mercy, I had the skinny one eat the chubby one's arse, holding her by the lank blonde hair so that she stuck to her task and feasted well. Cassie may well have come at this point but it was hard to tell as her cunt was so wet anyway. As my urgency gathered momentum I pushed Angel aside, grasped Cassie's hips hard and pierced her rump with the dildo at my waist. All she had to help her was slave-spit and her own secretions. I wish I could remember her cries more vividly but my head was almost bursting. I know it must have hurt her because I drove the toy deep from the very first thrust, wanting to feel that luscious slide as the clamping muscles are defeated and resistance evaporates. That first squash of your thighs against their soft bum is one of life's triumphs. You shudder with the delight of being the one stretching and filling their rude passage, of being the first to give that unmatched feeling of searing pain beneath sheer, unquantifiable pleasure.

Her rump danced, that I know. It slapped and juddered as I slammed against her, the flesh rippling in waves over the tortured cheeks. I fucked through my own huge release, plunging harder as my clit throbbed against the tight dildo harness. In the end my fury broke and left me exhausted as always, spent and sated. I collapsed on the bed, ordering them to get out and leave me alone. I needed calm after my storm and feared my own guilt should I wake up next to them. I was ever glad that sleep quickly obliterated my creeping remorse. Perhaps it would have been better if I'd never woken.

Angel was even quieter than normal over the next few days, ghosting around the house as if trying to avoid me and stave off the inevitable. I made her perform a couple of indignities but we both knew that her time with me was finished. She must have known my ravaging of that young body would only increase my desire for her rival, and she was right. Cassie had gone to ground but I wanted her more than ever. I was not unduly worried by her silent absence as she must have learnt that I prefer to give a long recovery time after my episodes. I prefer any proffered bottom to be pristine and I hate to be reminded of my lapses into uncontrolled lust. A good slave will always wait patiently to be summoned and soon enough I did this, calling on her in person and commanding her to be at my place when I came home from work the following evening. She nodded her compliance, but her head was bowed and she could barely look at me. It filled me with surging joy to see her so meek and mute.

I returned home just after the appointed hour, closing the door behind me and immediately sighting the trail of her discarded clothes leading me up the stairs. On the top step lay her white cotton knickers, carefully spread to show off their fullness, a hint of what was to come. As I turned towards my room there she was, my lovely Cassie naked and on all fours upon my bed, her big creamy rump thrust right out towards me, open and beckoning, both lewd and shyly subservient. To my delight she appeared to have healed well, with only some tell-tale bruising remaining at the tops of her thighs. Her bottom seemed its usual self: pale and unmarked, smooth and soft, and no doubt begging for more of my harsh treatment.

I had been starved of her arse those last few days and I was desperate to feed, to have the peach squashing into in my face as I pressed into her split to taste again that delicious little anus that I, and only I, had ever fucked. She knew I was there but she didn't turn to me, keeping her face down and hidden on the bed, surrendering herself to whatever I chose to visit upon her. I couldn't wait to hear her cry as I gripped her thighs and stuck my tongue right up her backside.

I saw the flash of skinny leg from behind the bedroom door but I had too much forward momentum to evade the contact at my shin. As I lifted my leg to hurdle it, the foot hooked around mine and rose to trip me. I went down heavy and sprawling. My arms splayed out to break the fall but skidded on the carpet. My chest thudded against the floor and knocked the wind from me. The skinny bitch was on me quick as a ferret, grabbing my feet to prevent me standing again and placing a foot on my arse to keep me flat.

Then I smelt the alien scent of orange blossom, the floral fug filling my nose as I sensed the mass just above me. The weight sat down upon my back and squeezed the last vestiges of air from my lungs. My hair was grasped and my head pulled back, a material strip perhaps from my own dressing gown forced between my lips like a gag. The belt was tied tight behind my head so that it bit into the corners of my mouth, and one end was left long so it could be held like a rein.

The orange blossom scent became stronger and the weight bore down at my back and shoulders and I could feel this new body right there at my ear, snarling about what a nasty cunt I was and how I was going to pay. The voice was full of spite but still carried an unmistakeable antipodean twang. I knew instantly that it belonged to big fat Jocelyn, summoned no doubt by her former slave to give protection and deal out justice – and by fuck did she!

My skirt was already being pulled off by that skinny, thankless bitch Angel. Jocelyn saw to my blouse, tugging it half open and dragging it down around my midriff, exposing my chest and helping secure my arms behind me. My underwear was snipped off with scissors and I could smell my own cunt, already pungent from thoughts of Cassie and mixed with the warmth of the evening. My struggles were utterly in vain. Although I roared my anger past the band in my mouth, Jocelyn's bulk pinned me to the floor and her sharply delivered slap to my face brought my stunned silence. I have *never* been beaten before, not even a few little smacks to see what it was like or to ascertain tolerances.

Jocelyn was now standing, tugging my head back with the rein she had fashioned whilst her bare foot pressed into my back to hold me down. It was Angel that administered this first beating, months and years of gathered bile spewing from inside her as she lashed my body with my own long-tailed whip. The tongues bit and wrapped around the exposed flesh on my legs and arse, giving no quarter despite my cries of pain. It was utterly vindictive. Between strikes she yelled obscenities at me and leaned over to send forceful gobs of spit into my face and hair. There was no mercy, the streaks of fire igniting my skin no matter how loudly I screamed. The belt forcing my mouth open prevented me from telling Angel that she was a cunt and that she was finished. However, she already knew the first part and would have disputed the second. The spite behind her thrashing told me she thought she was safe from me now. Her new Mistress backed this up with perfect timing, twisting my head hard to the side and pissing hotly onto it, not caring that her thick stream was drenching my carpet and must have been streaking her thighs.

Angel tossed the whip aside. I saw her grinning as she instead displayed and flexed the long cane I used whenever I lost control. I was hoping the whip had anaesthetised my arse but the line of fire she laid upon it eclipsed any pain I had ever felt. The panic was instant and gathered to hysteria in fractions of a second, but Jocelyn simply pressed her foot down harder and held me in place. Each stripe started cold, turning white hot and intolerable in an instant. Wriggling and screaming was no cure. My nerves had no way of coping, my surging adrenaline incapable of damping the fire. I dreaded the next stroke while my senses were still exploding from the last but, inexplicably, portions of as yet unpunished flesh fizzled as if advertising their desire to be the next target.

Angel did her best not to leave any part of my lower-half untouched, raining her revenge down upon the backs of my thighs and legs, down further to the defenceless portion just below my knees and the plump mounds of my calves. God help me, I even lifted my legs up to help her cane the soles of my feet. Did I really rake her with agony like this when I lost control? It was always so hard to remember what went on through my purple rages, although on some level I must have understood that despite the unbearable contact, your body still cried

162

out for more. Although my lungs seemed flat and unable to draw in air, although my saliva was oozing thick as retch past the belt in my mouth, even though my bowels were loose enough to all but yield control, some ridiculous part of me still prayed that each stroke was not the last. Jocelyn was bending over me now, trying to force a huge black dildo into my mouth, covering it in my saliva strings and wiping it over my piss-wet cheeks. Angel had ceased her beating and was goading her Mistress on to force the toy into my throat, to suffocate me with it. The aftershock of the beating was terrible, almost worse than the contact itself now that my nerve endings had a chance to bask in their agony. My hysteria could not relent either, not with my nose clogged with immovable snot and the plastic filling my mouth and seeming like it could choke me to death. Imagine being snuffed out, right here on my own urine-stained bedroom carpet, with little sign of a struggle and only the weight of a fat bitch to keep me in place! They would say it was an accident, and Angel would display her scarred and welted skin to prove it was just part of the games we liked to play.

My Cassie would save me though. She was trying to get my fat tormentor's attention, softly imploring to be heard from her place on the bed where she had stayed, presumably too wracked with guilt at her complicity in my plight to move. As the two bitches ravaged my throat with the dildo, I could hear her voice growing louder, demanding to be heard, I could feel her bouncing off the bed and pushing her way between their bodies to wrestle the toy from them.

'Give it to me!' she was saying, her voice hoarser and more forceful than I ever thought her capable of. 'Let me have my turn.'

I was so stunned by her treachery I offered no resistance as I was hauled up onto my knees. Angel was giving my backside a few smacks with her open palm but they barely registered, so engrossed was I with the sight of Cassie right at my side, donning the harness that now housed the grotesquely veined plastic cock. The head of it was still glistening from being forced down my throat. I watched a thick string of my own saliva, as viscous as any spunk-ooze, slowly drawing its way out from the dildo tip. It swayed lewdly in the air before its weight made it drip to the floor.

Cassie was in awe of the toy, gripping its shaft to feel the thickness fill her palm. She had to stretch her fingers to encompass the girth, the shiver visible over her whole body and her breath coming in fluttering gasps at the excitement of this new power at her waist. She got behind me and grasped my hips before I thought to struggle, but my efforts were way too late. Jocelyn put her hand to my neck and pushed me down, bringing one knee over me as my face squashed into the piss-drenched carpet so that she was facing Cassie behind me, her huge

164

arse pressing down on the back of my head to keep me pinned whilst her fat fingers grabbed both cheeks of my rump to hold them apart.

In my late teens I had once swapped dildo buggerings with my then girlfriend. That was just a careful, gentle slide as opposed to this hot-poker pain that seared in my anus and jagged lightning through my nerves. Once again the weight on top of me easily absorbed my screams and escape attempts. Ironically, the bowel-loosening terror that burst within me probably aided the slow passage of the fake cock inside me. I had precious little other help, my anus slickened only with the heat of the day and the coating of spit I had retched onto the toy.

I had often imagined as I sodomized my slaves what this excruciating experience must be like. I knew it was scintillating and incomparably intimate when done slow and deep with a long, very slender toy, and more delicious still, or so I was told, when taken up a dirty bum soon after evacuation. I always chose massive dildos for my slaves, and didn't care whether they wanted to shit themselves or not. And now it was my turn.

The hurt was immeasurable and doubled by the terror and realisation that avoidance was impossible. I knew that I had to make it stop but the toy was creeping millimetre by millimetre up my protesting backside and it felt like it was tearing me in two. I think I was screaming but I'm not sure if any noise was actually coming out, and if it was it was quickly doused by Jocelyn's backside. I needed to get away immediately. I tried to clear my head to reach into the flashes of bursting light and tumbling, panicked thoughts to grasp my safe-word and yell it. And then, with the same clarity as the white pain shooting through my arse, I remembered that I didn't *have* a safe-word. Until a few short moments before the whole idea of me ever needing one was utterly ridiculous. So I just had to take it.

My muscles slumped in defeat and my will crumpled, knowing everything I had strived to become had gone. Since those bitches took everything from me in that moment, I may as well let you into a secret: being bum-fucked by a huge, hard dildo makes you feel like you are being taken at your core, like your very soul is being fucked. It is that same terrible and beautiful feeling that a beating evokes; that same hot/cold malicious sting of the cane – but *inside* you this time. Each minuscule movement is an assault on your neurones but every jolt goes straight to your cunt, opening it up and making it stream, swelling your clit so that it might burst. It is simply beautiful. I wasn't quite sure if the pleasure came from within my rectum itself or from its proximity to my pussy and the friction against it caused by the monster filling me. All I know is that I came, massively – harder than ever because I had no way of checking it, no way to prevent the juggernaut crashing through my senses.

My tormentors stood over me and as I finally focused I got my first proper view of Jocelyn. Her hair was big, in jet-black rock-chick spikes, and I was a little shocked at how much prettier she was than I remembered, although this was in part due to her thick Goth make-up that accentuated her large eyes, high cheekbones and full lips. I never used to like the pronounced dimple in her chin, but now I saw it added authority to her looks. She was wearing a lace girdle to contain her belly rolls whilst her fat, snow-white tits threatened to spill over the top. Her rubber skirt was pulled up completely to expose her chubby, completely shaven cunt, her gash a deep, cute cut inside the smooth, puffy mons. It must be wonderful to have that squashed to your mouth. I was done now but she was not. She kicked my legs apart and put her foot to my saturated split, worming her podgy toes with their black glossed nails inside me. She pressed on and I gasped, defeated now and unable to prevent her from opening me up once more. I stretched for her and she slid inside. All five fat toes were within my hot puss, gently wriggling to make me squeal and to compound my humiliation. She took that foot out and showed it to me, so that I could witness the slick I had left there. Then she repeated the whole degrading process with her other foot.

I felt strangely calm and comforted, like an antelope calf in the jaws of a lion in those final seconds before death, when the endorphin release smothers the fright and all that is left is peaceful acceptance. I wanted to speak but the band still held my tongue. I wanted to piss, perhaps to let loose a shower all over them as a sign of my defiance, but more likely to crunch my belly muscles up so that my stream splashed all up my body and into my mouth to demonstrate my absolute surrender. She had decided that I wasn't quite beaten yet, or not quite beaten enough.

She had Angel bring her a long-handled paddle like a fly swat, and with a big smile on her pretty face, Jocelyn smacked my open cunt with it whilst the two other slaves were ordered to lick my come from the Mistress's toes. This time she didn't need to hold me down. I writhed and shrieked as my swollen lips bounced and slapped and jumped apart, but I stayed in position and took each stinging contact like the bitch I had become. After only ten or eleven strokes she cast her weapon aside, straddled me backwards, and sat her massive arse squarely down on my face.

I was lost in her cavernous crack, her slippery lips tight to mine and her anus pressed to my nose. The hot confines were airless and smelled of excitement and rudeness. It wouldn't take long before I was suffocated in there. It took me a while to make out her words as my head was just swimming. She was calling me her bitch and commanding that I swear fealty and yield to her.

She was demanding I consent to be her slave. I'm not absolutely sure, but I think I might have said yes, even without the threat of having my oxygen supply cut off. She dismounted and sent her other girls away, bending to whisper in my ear. My slaves belonged to her now, she told me, and she would return tomorrow to give me the terms under which I must now live.

Those terms are harsh and beyond my current comprehension. She came to my house and even let the meeting be conducted with me lying face down on the bed, since my backside is still too ravaged to allow me to sit. She spelled out her conditions one by one, each another dagger to my shrunken heart. I should have slapped her and called her a snivelling great pile of shit, a pitiful excuse for a Domme. I should have grabbed her by the hair and thrust my whole fist up her fat arse and then had her suck it clean. But I couldn't because without her I have nothing, I *am* nothing. I have no real sense now of where I begin or end.

My control has been ripped from me and against all my deepest instincts I just want to run to the cover of her. She knows too. She knows that I have no friends, no circle to fall back on. We both know that everyone will recoil further from me, will desert me completely, on hearing how I pillaged Cassie and rode roughshod over her safe-word. I have unforgivably violated the one promise of sanctuary that binds all of us in our world of

Mistress and Servant. Jocelyn knows that I am beyond being loved or even pitied now. She is my one chance of anything remotely resembling affection. Above all she knows that, even after all, I am besotted with Cassie, and only by becoming a fellow slave do I stand the chance to see and possibly touch her again.

I am to be the lowest of the low in Jocelyn's harem. No doubt buoyed by Angel's horror stories of things I made her do, I am to perform several unspeakable acts at my Mistress's whim. I am to undertake certain 'bathroom duties' as Mistress calls them, for her and possibly for the other slaves. In short, I am to lick her fat arse on a daily basis and worship her for it. Yes, I am now to be Daisy Everrlast, her Dirty Arse Slave, and I must change my name to prove it.

Gone is my power, gone is my free will. I am to be abused and debased in exchange for company and the fleeting hope that I will get to hold the one girl I think I truly loved and yet so despoiled. I am to be on the receiving end of all the filth I have dished out over the years and I can do nothing whatsoever, except on another's say so. The worst thing in all this – and this part absolutely withers me – is that I simply cannot keep my fingers out of my soggy cunt just thinking about it.

www.ingramcontent.com/pod-product-compliance
Ingram Content Group UK Ltd.
Pitfield, Milton Keynes, MK11 3LW, UK
UKHW022259180325
456436UK00003B/155